Moina's Heaven
&
Earth

Moina's Heaven
&
Earth

By Moina Morgan Vanderveer

Four Seasons Publishers
Titusville, FL

Moina's Heaven & Earth

This is a work of fiction.
All characters and events portrayed in this book are fictional, and any resemblance to real people is purely coincidental.

For information contact: Four Seasons Publishers
P.O.Box 51, Titusville, FL 32781

PRINTING HISTORY
First Printing 2000

ISBN 1-891929-31-3

PRINTED IN THE UNITED STATES OF AMERICA
1 2 3 4 5 6 7 8 9 10

Dedication

This book is dedicated to My Mother
No words, no matter how eloquently put, could pay her due homage.

Chapter I

Helen Terry's heart was heavy as she climbed the stairs leading to her bedroom. She was reluctant to take time out each day to rest, as her Doctor had ordered her to do.

Many months had passed since her first visit to the Doctor's office, and she was becoming very despondent over her still persisting condition. Well she remembered her Doctor's warning, today, as she climbed the stairs to her room. He had told her plainly enough her ultimatum: either she rest for a period each day, or her condition would become alarmingly acute.

Helen had listened intently, and had agreed to follow his directions to the letter. But as time went on she had found it more and more disturbing, as her condition failed to react satisfactorily to rest.

Today, especially, she wanted to feel well. It was her wedding anniversary, and she had hoped that once again she and Paul could celebrate in the old way. What jovial times they used to have together. Helen longed now to be well and her old self.

It seemed so long ago to her now, since she had been jovial and light hearted. How she had always loved all the parties that she attended, as well as gave. That was in the past. Of late she had been confined to a limited amount of activity, and even that, left her limp and tired.

Life hardly seemed worth the trouble to her as she laid her tired body down on the bed. Day after day, night after night, of endless waiting for full recovery. That once again she could take a more active part in the life all around her. She seemed so far removed from the world, and yet life went on for others in the usual manner. How much longer could she endure this life of inactivity, without becoming hopelessly drawn away from the outside world.

Her Doctor had warned her though, that unless she had this rest, she might one day be entirely incapacitated, or perhaps not live. Helen wanted to live, she was young. Yet the life of an invalid was not much better than death. These thoughts had oft times flashed through her mind of late. She was not much more than living death each day.

At any time, some over taxation of her heart might cause her death. That had been made very plain to her. She had, up to this time, been confident that with due care she would gain complete recovery. At times, she felt sure that she had gained ground, but today she felt hopelessly lost. The fatigue that overcame her was not growing any less, and she was discouraged. Today, of all days, she wanted to dance and be merry.

No doubt Paul was bored with living with one who was so lifeless, though he showed her nothing but the greatest consideration and kindness. How many times he had cheered her on, telling her of the many things -they would do when she was well again. Now on their fifth wedding anniversary, she would not be able to follow through with these long anticipated plans.

How tedious it must be for Paul, to live such a life of recluse. He was young and healthy, and loved good times. Always before, they had been the center of activity. People in for the evening, and going out together. Fully enjoying life, as only young people seem to have the knack, to grasp simple joys from otherwise common-place incidences. Such gaiety, they had always found together. Good times seemed to bloom wherever they were. It was as though they had sought it, but instead it flourished with out any great effort on their part. It had always been this way with the young Terry's, that is, until this heart ailment had overcome Helen. Since that time life went on for them, but the lights had gone out for Helen. Paul seemed to be his usual joyful self, in spite of the lessening of social activities that he loved so well; but Helen felt that it was somehow unfair to him.

She had tried one evening to tell Paul how she felt about the unjustness of making him suffer for her illness.

He had only laughed at her and had soon jollied her out of such a notion. He even told her that for the first time in his life, he was catching up on his reading. He really enjoyed this life of quiet relaxation, or so he told Helen.

All these things passed through Helen's mind as she lay on the bed. It was true that Paul seemed happy enough, but she surmised that he missed the good times as much as she did.

Now if she could get well. Time seemed long to her. It did seem, that with the constant care she had taken, she should be gaining ground. She was everlastingly tired, everything seemed such an effort and exhausting. At times it seemed to her, that she could not endure another day of this fatigue. Much better, she thought, to be right down good and sick, than this long drawn out torture of feeling so lifeless. A walking corpse, she had oftened likened herself to. She smiled to herself now, as she remembered voicing this thought to Paul. How well she remembered the look that came over his face, and then his reprimanding her for even suggesting that he was, or could be, in love with a corpse, whether walking or otherwise. He told her that he was very much in love with her and so such a possibility of her resembling any kind of corpse was out of the question.

It was a good thing for Helen these days that Paul was so easily filled with mirth, as he did a lot in this way to encourage her on. It was hard to stay despondent with him around. Helen was far from the moody type herself, but at times in the past months she had been overcome with a feeling of futility.

Helen lying on the bed, half asleep and half awake, let these thoughts flow through her mind, and began to relax.

It did not seem to her that she had dropped to sleep, but all at once she felt very refreshed, as though she had had a long rest. Rested to a greater extent that she had remembered for a long time back. It was almost unbelievable that she could feel so well again. Could it be that she had slept. It hadn't seemed to her that she had, yet she felt entirely rested. She felt as she had, before this illness had become a part of her life. Never had she remembered feeling any better than she did at that moment. Strange that her recovery should come about so abruptly, when she had been feeling worse that day than usual. The urge to get up and be active filled her. She had been told to lie down each day for two hours at least. Certainly she hadn't rested for more than thirty minutes, and still she felt so well that she must get up. Energy, and the desire to be active surged through every part of her body. Surely there was no reason for lying down when she felt so well. All the tiredness had vanished as if by magic. Helen sat up on the edge of the bed and smiled to herself. It was as though a heavy weight had been lifted from her and she was free once more to take up life.

"I feel so wonderful!" she said aloud.

Her own voice startled her in the quietness of the house.

"I'm not in the habit of talking to myself, but as long as I feel so well, who cares! Perhaps it is the shock of feeling so well again." Helen laughed. "They say, only the very old or foolish talk to themselves. Well, I certainly do not feel old now. I may be a bit giddy from the sudden feeling of well being, but I hardly think I have taken loss of my senses."

It seemed to amuse Helen to be talking to herself this way. She would enjoy telling Paul of how she had quite a chat with herself. He would laugh at her and in mock seriousness suggest she see a Doctor.

Helen stretched her arms high over her head and looked pleased with herself. There was a twinkle in her eyes as if some mischief was in her mind. Her face radiated life. She was almost afraid to move about for fear the old pangs of her illness would return.

"Oh I don't know when I have felt as well as this!

Perhaps after all, Paul and I will, celebrate our anniversary. I see no reason why we shouldn't, if I continue to feel this well. It would be foolish not to, when I am feeling better than I can ever remember of feeling before. Perhaps this is my reward for all the care I have taken. I wonder if the Doctor knew it would happen this way. At any rate, I am going to take advantage of this bouyancy while it lasts, it is too wonderful to waste sitting around."

Helen walked over to her dressing table. She would pretty herself up and prepare a special dinner for Paul. Then, if she still felt so abundantly well, she and Paul would step out for the evening in celebration of their anniversary.

Paul would be surprised to see her so well. She thought he would be able to see it at a glance. He wouldn't be able to help but notice the great difference, as she could feel it radiating from every part of her. She would put on her best dress, but first she must fix her hair.

Helen was making plans and was a bit surprised at the excitement she felt over her sudden recovery. She had been carried away with plans for the evening, but brought her mind back to concentrate on what she started out to do.

Helen smiled happily as she reached for the comb that lay on her dressing table. She placed her hand over it, dreamily smiling over her sudden joy of being well again.

Her smile faded in a moment. Helen was astonished. She had hand on the comb, but could not seem to pick it up. She was bewildered. She tried again. That was strange, she could not pick up the comb. Certainly she was not dreaming. She couldn't be, she was wide awake, that she knew.

But, what could be the matter with the use of her hand, that she found herself unable to lift the comb. She carefully placed her hand over it and clutched the comb, but it did not budge. She never heard of anything so rediculous. She never felt so entirely well as she did at that moment, and yet; she could not lift that comb. Her hand did not seem to be asleep, but perhaps it was. She wiggled her hand open and shut. It functioned perfectly. She moved her arm back and forth, and then lifted it up in the air. There didn't seem to be anything the matter with her, until she tried to lift the comb.

"Well! I never!" she said aloud.

She tried once more. She was becoming more and more bewildered, and a bit panicky. Finally she gave up and decided to arrange her hair as best she could with her hands. Perhaps later she could comb it.

She glanced into the mirror to see how she was making out, and let out a gasp. There was no reflection of herself in the mirror and she knew that she was standing directly in front of the glass. She must be dreaming. She knew it had been too good to be true, this feeling of well being. She had a moment ago, such great hopes that she had recovered from her long illness, but it was turning out to be a hideous nightmare. Baffled and keenly disappointed, she turned away from her dressing table.

As she turned she noticed someone standing by her side. Her disappointment was so keen, that she gave little notice. It did not occur to her right then, that she had been in the room alone. Her mind was turning over the incidents of the past few moments. Suddenly, this realization came over her, and she looked again at the person beside her.

"Mother! I never was so glad to see anyone in my life! How did you get here? I didn't hear you come in, but I was so preoccupied. I had the most terrible experience a moment ago. I was feeling so wonderfully well Wait a minute.

What is the matter with me? Have I taken loss of my senses? Mother it can't be you! Yet it is. Why— Why— you are just as you ever were. But how can it be? You are dead.I had forgotten that for a moment. I was startled to see you. It seemed just natural to have you walk in. Yet, I do not understand. Now that I stop to think, I know, that you are dead, and still, here you are with me, just exactly as you always were. I can't understand the things that are happening today."

Helen's mother came over to her and embraced her. "Yes Helen, it is rather baffling, the experience you just went through. I was watching you and waiting for you to notice me. I didn't want to startle you, I wanted it to come about naturally."

Helen grasp her mother's arm. "Why mother it is you! In the flesh." "How did you expect me to be?" Helen's mother said, laughing at her daughter's surprise at finding her unchanged.

"I don't know, I really don't know. But how is it that I can see you, feel you, and hear you? I have never seen you before in all the years you have been dead. Now it is just like before, before the day you died, and just as natural and real. You are dead? Yes, I know you are. Yet- "

"Yet, you can't see how I can be dead, and so very much alive. Is that it?" she said, smiling at her daughter. "Well you see the truth is, when we are dead, as you call us, we are in reality very much more alive than we were in our earth life. That is to say, we lose all our earthly hindrances, such as physical ills and handicaps brought on by earth's demands on our physical bodies. When we are released from our body, we are unencumbered by these physical drawbacks. Therefore, we feel very much more alive than we did while on earth, because we have perfect health and thus lose the restrictions that befall us in our earth life. Now do you see why I am still very much alive after shedding my cloak of that earthly body? It is no more than a cloak, you know, and we shed it as easily, only changing our garment."

Helen was looking off into space, but taking in every word her mother was saying. A thought was toying in her mind as she listened.

Now, Helen looked at her mother. Her lips parted as though she was about to speak. She looked perplexed, as if some thought that had gone through her mind was too preposterous to even voice.

Finally she said, slowly, hesitatingly, almost afraid to voice her thoughts, "Mother.. could that be.. is that why I feel so much better physically, so buoyant and unhampered? Is that why I couldn't see myself in the mirror, nor pick up the comb?"

Helen had voiced these thoughts now, and seemed relieved. Yet she couldn't be dead. Her body was the same and she herself seemed unchanged. She had the same reactions, the same personality, the same mannerisms, that made her the person she was.

Yet, so did her mother seem the same. Death had not changed her in any way. She still retained all of her little ways that were so dear to Helen.

She looked closely at her mother again, as if to verify this. She was just the same, except, in a way. She hadn't noticed any change at first, but now she could see her mother had lost the worn tired look. No tired lines, nor look of fatigue to mar her lovliness. But, other than that, Helen could see no signs that would mark her as changed in any way.

"Why do you stare at me so? Do I look like a ghost to you?" She laughed, as she said this.

"No mother, I was only trying to see if I could find something about you that had changed through death." "And what did you find? Helen smiled and hugged her mother tightly. "Nothing, you are just as real a mother as you ever were, only more beautiful."

"Go along with your blarney. I used to be taken in with your soft talk, but I am wise to your methods now," said Helen's mother, glad once more to be chatting with her daughter.

"But mother, am I dead too? I must be, to explain all that is happening. Yet I really can't be."

"By that so you mean that because you do not feel dead, or because you do not like the idea of being dead?" she asked her daughter, uneasily.

"I don't know, the idea is all so new to me", replied Helen. "I don't feel as though I were dead, but neither do you. It's not that I dislike being dead, if it's like this, but it's for Paul's sake."

"Yes that is the way we all feel when our time comes. Glad for ourselves, only regretful because of those we leave behind on earth, who do not understand that we go on living, very much the same as we did on earth. Yes my dear, that is our only disappointment when we leave our earthly body. You asked me if you were dead. You are the same as you would be, if you were dead, but whether you remain with us, is questionable."

"But mother, if I am not dead, how can I be here with you? Certainly this is no dream. If I am dead, tell me. I have to know sooner or later, do not try to save me from the truth. When a person is dead, how can there be, any question about his remaining dead?"

"Well my daughter, you will know sooner or later, just as I will. But, at the moment, as I told you, you are not in a true sense dead. You are out of your physical body, that is true, and you are just as you would find yourself if you were to stay out of that physical body for all time. The only difference now, is that your life cord has not been broken from your body. As long as that remains strong, and is not detached, there is every possibility that you may return to live again in your physical body. That is dependent on whether or not your physical body is strong enough to carry on through your illness."

"Where is this life cord you are speaking of? I don't feel anything holding me, nor do I see any cord."

"It is there, Helen, nevertheless. You just don't recognize it. If you knew what to look for, you could see it."

"Do you see it, Mother?"

"Yes, I can see it, and that is why I know you are only released from your body, and as yet, have not transgressed permanently into this world."

"Please show it to me, mother."

"Look over toward the bed, and in direct line from you as you are now, you will see a very brightly lighted cord leading to your body there on the bed. It will be about as large as a small rope, and its brightness will resemble the rays of the sun. It is power given to man by God, to keep his body and soul together. When this cord is nonexistent, then complete death has occurred. As long as your body is able to function properly, or the time for you to leave earth life, comes, that life cord is the power that keeps your soul housed in your physical body. Your physical body is the means by which you are allowed to take an active part in earth life. When that body is no longer useful, then your soul is released so that you may take up your new life in God's world."

"Then perhaps I am only here on a visit. There is a chance that I may return to my physical body, and live on earth again. Does anyone know, what the outcome will be?" Helen asked.

"Only Divine power knows the outcome of this experiment, and we do not question His Wisdom. Now turn and see if you can see the life cord. But, remember also, to be prepared to see your physical body on the bed."

Helen turned slowly around. She was preparing herself for the shock of seeing her body lying on the bed. First she was attracted by the brightly lighted cord, that was in size like a small rope. It was so much brighter and more radiant than any light she had ever seen. It filled her with reverence as she gazed upon it, as she could feel its overwhelming power. Then she saw her body lying on the bed. She was amazed to find how perfectly natural it all seemed, to be standing there looking down at her body. It was no more of a shock than looking in the mirror, but just as disappointing. She smiled and turned to her mother.

"I am not at all flattered to see that physical body of mine. Someway it seemed to reflect more satisfactorily in my mirror when I was all prettied up, but perhaps I wore rose colored glasses."

"Helen's mother laughed with Helen. She too had looked at her worn out body a long time ago, and had felt very much the same way.

"I am not so sure!" said Helen, "that I will care to crawl back into that body. What are all those people doing around the bed? Some of them look like Doctors in those white uniforms. What are they doing to my body? I seem to be breathing, that is, my body is still breathing. This is rather confusing, with two of me to think about."

"Yes," said Helen's mother, "this is a strange experience for you. Those men are Doctors, Doctors with great knowledge. They have been sent from the highest realms of Heaven to heal your sick body. They are going to try to make your body function properly again. If they are successful, you will return to earth life and once more be housed by your physical body; if not, the life cord will be removed, and all its power gone. You are now what is known on earth as, in a coma. Your body is functioning, but you are not conscious. The conscious part of you has left the body, and is standing here looking on. The real you, has left its housing. They will take care of your body and notify us if they want you. Come, let's leave, I have a great deal to show you before you return to earth life."

Helen was intently watching the Doctors. It was fascinating to see them work, but it was true that she could be of no help, so she followed her mother.

Chapter II

As they left the house, they were met by Helen's father who greeted his daughter warmly. It was a treat to have his daughter with them again, and he had so many things of wonder in store for her. Things he knew would be a delight and a revelation to her.

The three of them chatted, as they made their way from the earth surroundings. Helen marveled at the means of travel. They walked, or so it seemed to her, yet they covered a great amount of territory in such a little space of time. Helen spoke of this to her parents.

"That is only the first wonder of this world of ours,"said her father. We travel vast distances in moments. It seems like magic until you have been here for awhile, and then it seems quite common-place. It is like getting used to anything. Automobiles for instance, they seemed pretty speedy at first, but soon people wanted to drive faster. You will see a great many things unfold before your eyes that will be difficult for you to understand at first. But if you accept them as you find them, perhaps before you return to earth you will understand them more fully."

"What no wings! Nor golden chariots!? asked Helen, in mock seriousness. "What a disappointment for all the people who expect to be met by a golden chariot and be driven off to Heaven."

"No, but that is only one of the mistaken ideas that you people on earth have dreamed up," said Helen's father. We neither have wings, nor are we angels. We are exactly the same sort of person that we were while we lived on earth. The mere shedding of our earthly body does not change us as a person. No one would expect to see much real change in himself nor suddenly become a better person by merely changing his clothing. Yet someway they expect when they step out of their physical body, to suddenly become an entirely different person. We are in reality, only what we have made of ourselves while living on earth. We are absolutely unchanged as you can see with your own eyes. However we can better ourselves as a person, if we choose to. In due time, most everyone who comes into this wonderful world, where he is unhampered, does strive to further and widen his scope. There are a few, and a very few, who have no desire at all to progress and learn. That is entirely up to the individual, just as it is in earth life. Your mother and I have learned many wonderful things while we have been here, but have not accomplished all that we desire. We are forever seeking new beauties of this land, and an understanding that can only come with time. You see we haven't gained so much knowledge that you mistook us for a stranger. You still recognized us and feel very much at home with us."

"You haven't changed a bit, father, you are just as modest as ever, just as big a joker, and I love you for it," Helen replied. "I hardly believe that I would care much for you as parents, if I found you had sprouted wings. It just doesn't seem to appeal to me someway."

"That's right dear," said Helen's mother. Some way it is a great joy, for us to come over here and find those we know, unchanged. Oh in time, we lose some of our faults and petty ways as we grow less selfish and self-centered, but as a whole we are quite the same. You will notice this by the way we live. We live very much in the same manner that we did on earth, having our homes, friends and outside activities. Our interest in things vary as to our likes and dislikes just as they did when we were on earth. We do not all care for the same things here, any more than we all liked the same things on earth. One man's delight is not necessarily that of another. We want you to see how we live with your own eyes, so that when you go back to Earth you will think of us as living a happy life. We want you to understand our ways as much as you can before you leave, so that you will have this truth to take back with you."

"Now," said Helen's father, "we are coming into the sphere in which we live. Look about you. What do you think of it?"

Helen looked about. It was beautiful, more beautiful than her parents had led her to believe. Not in the flimsy sort of way that she had always pictured her idea of Heaven, but very real and solid. It was a world as real as earth, but beautiful, beyond description. No golden streets, nor pearly gates with angels fluttering about, but perfection as only could be found in Heaven. Earth with all its beautiful buildings and places of beauty to see, would in comparison to this world that Helen was now seeing, look shabby and drab. The color and architectural designs of the building she saw made her stand in awe. She had never dreamed of such beauty.

Her father touched her on the arm, “So you like it?” he asked, knowing well the feeling that had come over her.

“I never in all my life imagined such beauty!” said Helen, still sort of entranced by it all. “Look at those roses! How full bloomed they are, and the colors!” She reached down and held one in her hand. “May I pick it” she asked.

“If you wish”, said her mother, but we have many more of them in our own yard”.

Helen was reluctant to leave the flowers behind, for fear that the others would not be quite as lovely as these.

Her parents smiled at each other, knowing so well the overwhelming desire of their daughter to drink in all this new found beauty. They expected her to react this this way, and therefore let her take her time to marvel at the sights that fell before her eyes, as they walked along the street.

Helen hardly knew where to look first. Things were not really so different, except for their outstanding beauty. There were streets, just as in any city or village. Trees in beautiful array of all kinds. Flowers of all varieties, and the grass was like a carpet of green without any unsightly brown dry spots.

Helen spoke to her father of the material used in the buildings. “They resemble in some ways, materials we have on earth, but still there is a difference. The stone has such delicate colors and seems to be embossed. Then there is other material used here that I cannot even try to name, but

I recognize brick, stone, marble and slate or something that is likened to these. Yet I can see that they are somewhat different than what we know on earth."

"Yes, Helen, you will find many things here that are familiar in a sense, but in reality they are entirely of a different substance than you have on earth. That is because of our atmospheric conditions, of which you will learn more about later."

They passed a group of children along the way and Helen smiled at them. They seemed to be having a good time playing some sort of a game in a group on the lawn. There was a sky overhead and sunlight all around. How very much like earth, and yet so different. The same familiar sights, only so far superior. Large buildings and small buildings. Churches, schools, libraries, homes and recreation centers. Yes, a great deal like earth, and fortunate too, for it was compelling enough just to grasp the beauty, that seemed so abundant everywhere.

Helen heard music coming from the doors of a Cathedral as she passed by. The beauty and reality of this world filled Helen with intentness. She felt she wanted to absorb all that she saw so that she could keep a picture of it in her mind forever. One thing that stood out in her mind, was the lack of any sordidness and disorder. It had the appearance of being brand new. Time had not left its mark on this world, and yet it was as old as time itself. This world had always been and was everlasting. Strange how clean and bright it was. There was dirt for the flowers and trees to grow in, but it didn't seem to be dirty dirt, the kind one tracks around on one's feet. Helen could not understand this, and it could not be explained to her. It was one of the many many things of God's designing in His world of perfection, and taken for granted by those who dwell there.

As they passed an orchard, Helen's father asked her to notice that there was no fruit laying on the ground. "That", he said, is also one of the laws of the land. On earth when fruit becomes ripened and falls to the ground, it rots. Here when fruit is not eaten quickly enough and it falls to the ground, it is immediately decomposed and taken from sight, leaving no disorder on the ground. Disorder and uncleanliness is not permitted to exist here."

Helen was beginning now, to learn of the laws that governed everyone and everything in this beautiful land. One learned almost instinctively the laws of God, and reverently abided by them. It was in the air and all around her. She could feel the power that focused on every living thing. She could feel the power of Divine creation, as one would sense the vastness of a forest, or the freshness in the spring air. Other than that, it was hard to explain just how one became so aware of this magnetic power. It seemed to penetrate deep into the soul, as a law voiced. Helen by this time was feeling this power so strong all around her, that there was no question in her mind, of a Supreme power that ruled Heaven and Earth. As she became more conscious of it, she spoke to her parents about it.

"So you are beginning to feel the Divine Power that rules our world so closely", said her father. "I thought perhaps you had not been made aware of it yet."

"I thought it must be, as I kept feeling it stronger and stronger but I wasn't sure just what it was. I have been enjoying the beauty of this land so much, that I hadn't gotten around to ask many questions about God. I always imagined that that would be the first thing I would do when

I got to Heaven, be taken to God."

Helen's parents understood, for was not that the idea of earth people in connection with dying. They expected to go directly to the father on high.

This was truly going to be difficult to explain to their daughter. Perhaps one of the most difficult things of all, that they would be called on to clarify for her. It was a delicate thing to understand, even after many years of living in the Heavenly sphere. God was all about, ever powerful. One felt His presence wherever he went, oft times directed by thought, as to the right course to follow. Still one did not see him, the great Divine Power that was master over every living thing in Heaven and Earth.

In the world of souls, unhampered by the physical body and earthly surroundings, it was natural to feel the presence of this Power, ever around, like a bright warm ray flooding through your very being. It was not necessary to see him, when you could feel his presence and be guided by his thought. It was not a thing of mystery nor question, once you learned to take it for granted. Understanding of his wondrous ways, comes about naturally in the course of time, as you live in daily contact with His ever presence.

Helen could feel that this was all so true, and although she could not quite grasp it fully, in such a brief glimpse into this new world, she could feel it all about her.

"Then if I were really to stay here, I would not go to God and be judged?" she asked.

"No," her father told her. "You are your own judge, for you see so clearly all your shortcomings, when you are fully released from your earth body. You are still of earth, and so do not as yet, experience this. When full and complete death takes place, it is only a short time before that soul knows all his failings, while on his mission to earth. He becomes conscious of his sins and failure to do, that which was his to do. No one tells him nor reprimands him; he sees only too clearly his own mistakes, and is justly punished through his own grief. If he is overcome by this grief and is desirous to make amends, he is shown how he can accomplish this. Until this desire is sincere and forceful, he is restricted. Restricted in the extent that he is allowed to do, and to have. All privileges are not granted him until he has righted, through his own effort, the wrongs that he has committed against himself, or others, while on Earth. Only then, is he allowed to progress and enjoy, without limitation, all of God's great land. Some people are fully content with these limitations, and do not care to progress. That is entirely up to them. Many years, sometimes pass, before they have any desire to enjoy the abundant privileges that can be theirs. That is just as true here as it is on earth. Some people here, as on earth, do not strive to reach higher goals. They are perfectly content with their status. Others are eager for knowledge, and delve deeply into the study, for progression of their souls. It depends largely on the individual. Some find this world such an improvement over earth life, even in the lowest realms, that they have little inclination to better themselves. There is no law that forces progression upon them. They are only limited by the scope of the sphere they are in, not being permitted to view beyond the limits of their deserving. There is no limitation of the things to be learned here. It is only in time that we learn how true this is. Constantly new opportunities are shown and taught to us, as we reach out for progression. As a rule, the more we learn of the unlimited possibilities of this land, the more eager and hungry for knowledge we become. The desire to be worthy of the privileges of the higher realms, opens the way for us, as we seek our goal. You will understand this, more and more, if you remain here. "

Helen walked along, listening with great interest, and taking in all the beauties that opened before her.

A bird on the wing, caught her eye. Strange, she hadn't thought much about the animals before. This was not the first, she had seen since coming, but it was only now, that she became conscious of it. Now she rembered, having seen birds back by the flowers, and also squirrels frisking up the trees. It had been so natural to see them, that she gave it little thought at the time.

Except for the outstanding beauty, things seemed very natural to Helen. It was hard to realize that she was with the dead. She smiled. The dead, yet so very much alive and living normal lives, just as the earth people. It was the perfect way to have it. And yet, people on earth imagined it to be so differently. How lost one would be, to find himself in unfamiliar surroundings. Supposing, she had wings and flew about. She certainly wouldn't feel very normal. Such a radical change would be too baffling. Much better, she thought, to remain the same, enjoying to the utmost the better existing in this place of beauty. It had been planned well, thought Helen.

Death was so easy and natural. There really didn't seem much to it, after all. It was just a case of discarding a body as one would an old shoe, no longer of any use to him. No feeling of fear, nor hurt. Fact was, she had left her body without any knowledge of having done so. Why then, did people talk of the tortures of death, and of the struggle. Helen knew now that death knew no pain. Pain, had to do only with the physical part of you, your body. Only while in that body, was it possible to suffer physically. The agony of pain was in reality, the process of living. Living was what made one suffer; and not dying. Dying was a release from all that, as Helen had learned so recently. Strange, that she had never thought of it before, but people suffered greatly during a sickness, that they later recovered from. If they had not recovered and lived on in the physical body; this undoubtedly, would have been called the suffering of death, which was not true at all. Death comes about as peacefully, as one awakens from a restful sleep. and with no more discomfort.

Helen was glad to be out of her tired body and free from its discomforts. Other than this, she did not feel its lack. She had, what appeared to her, the same body. It looked the same, felt the same, and functioned in its use the same as her physical body had. Only now she was not ill, nor tired. She looked down at herself as if to make sure. She was all intact. She smiled, after looking herself all over. Just the same, only much better, she thought. It was just like getting all dressed up in your finest togs, after having on a crumpled housedress. It was no more than a change of clothing. She, herself, had not been changed in any way. She was enjoying her new freedom, and was not so sure that she would want to return to earth, and her physical body.

It was a pleasure to walk and talk again with her parents. She had missed their companionship, and this seemed like old times. She knew now, that they lived on, only removed from her earth life. She knew that they were happy and would not want to live again on earth. When, and if, she returned to earth, she would have this thought to comfort her, until she too could join them again.

Chapter III

Helen's thoughts had wandered, as they made their way through the streets. Now she was aware that they had reached their destination, as they stopped to turn up the walk leading into a house.

"Is this where you live?" Helen stood in admiration. "What a lovely place!" It seems made, just for you, your dream come true. But the material? What is it?" Helen reached out and touched it, as though it might give her some conception of its kind. "It looks like stone. Still, it can't be compared to stone that I was familiar with on earth. It has such depth, and color. I have noticed, so often, the coloring over here. Colors outstandingly different than we have on earth. Some of them fit in with our colors, but others, to my mind, have no category."

"That is because they are Heavenly colors," Helen's mother explained. "You have some of our colors, but in different hues. These particular colors, exist no other place. You would find if you traveled around this world, from sphere to sphere, that the colors and materials vary a great deal. The higher one progresses, the greater difference one finds. Also, on the lower spheres, or planes, as we call our levels of living, you would find a great deal of difference in textures and materials used, as well as in coloring. We hope, while you are here, to show you some of the different planes. You will not be permitted to see them all, but we can show you a great deal in our own surroundings, and on the lower planes."

Helen's father opened the door and ushered her in.

A burst of "Surprise! Surprise!" greeted Helen.

There gathered together, waiting for her arrival, were some of her relatives. They had gathered, to celebrate Helen's homecoming, and were jubilant as they greeted her.

Helen was pleased and very much surprised to see those that she knew so well. She was confused for a moment in all the commotion of greetings, but soon regained her composure. The party in her honor was so unexpected that it overwhelmed her for a moment.

Helen had been so intent, since coming on this visit, that she hadn't thought to inquire about her relatives. There had been so much to take up her attention along the way, that the natural questions had been put aside.

Uncle Harry was the first to reach her side, and gave her a hearty welcome.

Then he said, "We thought you were never going to get through gaping around, and get here."

"How did you know I was gaping around; if you were

waiting here to surprise me?" Helen asked flippantly.

"Well it is plain to see that you haven't learned much of our ways," Uncle Henry teased. "We wondered what could be keeping you so long, so we investigated, and found you gaping at everything along the way. So we made up our minds to settle down for a long wait, seeing how you seemed so curious. Then too, your mother sent us word that you would be delayed a bit."

Helen turned to her mother, "When did you send them a message? You never left my sight," she asked, bewildered.

Helen looked so taken back, and surprised to find they knew what she had been doing, that they couldn't help but laugh. It was not that they expected her to understand their phenomena in such a brief period; but it was rather like having a small child ask some simple question, that one with more knowledge, knew the answer to so well. It was not so much the question, as her attitude that amused them.

"No I didn't leave your side", said Helen's mother, sobering now. "And don't let them make fun of you. They didn't always know the answer, either. They were just as baffled as you are. When I found that we were going to be longer than we anticipated, I did, however, send them word."

Uncle Henry broke in again, "Here, let me explain it to her. I started it, and I guess I got myself into a job. Here, Helen, sit here by me. Perhaps the best way would be to demonstrate to you. First of all, though, I will let you in on a little secret," he whispered in her ear.

Helen laughed as Henry whispered to her. "Not really?"

she said.

"Yes it is a fact, here I'll show you," he said.

"What are you two up to," said Helen's father, as he watched the two of them with their heads close together, and very apparently having the time of their lives.

"Never you mind now, we are quite busy. Are you ready now to try it, Helen?" Uncle Henry asked.

"Sure, go ahead," Helen replied, with a twinkle of interest in her eyes.

Uncle Henry sat looking at Helen, grinning from ear to ear. It had been quite some time since he had had the opportunity to show off to any newcomers, and he was thoroughly enjoying himself.

"It works!" Helen shouted with glee. "Try it again, this is fun."

"First", said Uncle Henry, "tell me what thought I sent you."

"You said, now, do you believe that your mother sent me the message!" repeated Helen.

"Well, do you?" asked Uncle Henry.

"How can I doubt it, when I got your thought? But can you do it as easily at a distance?" she asked.

"It works just the same, no matter where you might be. It is like a spoken word coming over the radio. It can be heard here, as well as at a distance," Uncle Henry explained.

You said it was like a spoken word. Yet, mother and the rest here, did not hear it, only I heard it," Helen said, thinking she had hit upon a flaw.

Helen's mother interrupted here, "thoughts are spoken words, that is true, but only if the thought is directed to you. This afternoon, I directed my thought to the folks gathered here waiting for me. I didn't want you to know, so I did not direct this thought to you, as I wanted you to be surprised. You can imagine how very confusing it would be, if all thoughts, were as spoken words to everyone in this world. Therefore, they are only heard by those who we wish to send the thought. It would be quite distracting right now, if we were to hear all the thoughts of those who live in this world. And, besides, there are those in earth life, that are also sending out thoughts that penetrate into this world, but as they are not meant for us, we do not receive them. That is one of the laws that rule the Universe, and thankful we are for it. But come, we must not try to fill you too full of knowledge at one time. Now then, you know your Aunt Linda, Uncle Frank you know well, Cousin Mary here, and your maternal and paternal grandparents!"

"Yes, and I am so glad to be with you again. You are all just as I remembered you!" Helen walked over to her grandmother. "Well Granny, I see that you still wear your little white apron."

"Yes, Helen, and I wouldn't feel right without it. I guess we hold pretty much to our peculiar little ways, no matter where we live. I suppose it is rather silly and useless, but it is a habit of long standing and I enjoy wearing it," she said, smiling lovingly at Helen. Helen leaned down and kissed her granny on the cheek. She had always loved her dearly. The little white apron tied around her Grandmother's tiny waist was familiar to her. As long as she could remember, it had been a part of her grandmother's habitual dress, especially, these dainty little aprons, when she entertained guests at tea. Helen smiled, when she remembered how many times they had all gathered like this on earth at her Grandmother's house, for a family reunion. Well, this was a family reunion, and they were all just the same, joking and full of fun. Helen had to stop and think to realize that they were no longer of earth. She could hardly believe that they were so unchanged by death. This was truly an experience to be grateful for.

"I am certainly glad that you were altogether like this," Helen told them. "You will never know how very much it has pleased me, this party in my honor."

"Pleased you!" Uncle Frank said. "Why, when someone from earth is coming over, we make big plans for it. We call a holiday and halt all our activities to welcome you home. It is a happy occasion as you can well see."

"It certainly is," said Helen. "Death to you is a time to rejoice, while on earth, it is a time of sorrowing."

"After all," said Uncle Henry, "Why shouldn't we be happy. My goodness sakes alive, when someone comes home after a long time away, aren't you glad to see them? We get just as lonesome to have you with us now, as we did when we didn't see you for a a long time when we were on earth. Why, we look forward to the day that you die, just as a kid looks forward to Christmas. And I might add. that we get just as excited. in your case, it is even more joyous, as you may go back to earth life."

"How do you know that?" Helen asked.

"Well bless my soul. Don't you think that I can tell a soul that has the marks of earth still clinging to it. It stands out like a light in the dark," Uncle Henry told her teasingly.

"Do you mean, that anyone who sees me can tell that I am not to stay here?" Helen asked. "I look just like the rest of you. I have no earthly body. I am just as much spirit or soul, what ever you call us when we no longer live in our physical body, as the rest of you."

"Yes," said Helen's father, but have you forgotten about the life cord that your mother told you about?"

Helen laughed. "Yes I had forgotten about it. I guess with such a bright ray of light as that casting from me, everyone who sees me will know that I am only on a visit."

"All who see you will know that you are one of the few who have such a great privilege. It is something to be proud of, for only occasionally, are earth people granted this special treat of glimpsing our beautiful world of souls," said her father.

"Come Helen," said Aunt Linda, "We have another treat for you. We have prepared a feast in your honor."

"Food?" asked Helen. "That sounds good to me. Now that you mention it, I realize that I haven't eaten for quite some time and am hungry."

"That is because you are still of earth. For some time after entering this world you feel the pangs of hunger, but after a while you do not require food so often. We have foods that suits our needs. Your grandfather and I do not require as much food as your parents do, as we have been here much longer and therefore have learned that we do not require it in such great amounts," said Helen's Grandmother, "although we do enjoy it, on a festive occasion such as this. Come, we will let you taste our food and see what you think of it."

Helen went with the others into the dining room where a table was set in banquet style. A center piece of flowers from her father's own garden graced the table. Helen stood in admiration as she glanced over the display of food. The table was filled with such an assortment of food as Helen had never known. There were fruit juices in abundance, figs, sliced fruit, berries, vegetables of the green variety and nectars, as they called them. There were things on the table that were strange to Helen, but she relished the taste of them. Helen partook of delicacies resembling pastries, but quite different than anything she had ever eaten before. She enjoyed the food and ate heartily.

The others enjoyed the feast, and told Helen the names of the foods that she was unfamiliar with.

"We do not have meat," said her father. "That is forbidden here, but we do not require it as the physical body of earth does. The animals here are of spirit, and so would not serve the purpose as they do on earth, as was intended. Our diet consists mostly of fruits, vegetables and nectars, as you see. We are adequately supplied by Divine Power and want for nothing that our souls require."

Each, in turn, added a bit of enlightenment on the subject, so that Helen could better understand the ways and needs of the living dead. They also gave her an advanced idea of some of the things that she would witness during her stay with them.

The house was full of activity and laughter. It was truly a jovial celebration for Helen's visit. In the midst of it all, Helen couldn't help but compare their happiness at having her there; with the mourning that took place on earth when one left his physical body. Helen could now see both sides of it, and fully realized that it was only a matter of view-point. It was no more than normal for each to react accordingly.

The meal finished; they returned to the living room to visit. "Now, what would be of interest to you, Helen?" her mother asked. "Oh I Would like to learn more about speaking silently, or thought projection I guess you called it."

"It might do you some good at that,"said Aunt Linda. Maybe when you go back to live on earth, you will pay more attention to us when we come to call on you."

"Oh, do you come to call on me?" asked Helen, quite surprised. "Many, many times. That is the main use of this thought projection. We only use it here, when we are not with someone whom we wish to speak to, then we send them the thought. Otherwise, we use on power of speech just as you do. Thought projection is used more to contact the minds of those who still live on earth.

We are able in this way to help them a great deal, although they may not realize it," said Aunt Linda.

"Have you given me a thought this way when I was in my physical body?" Helen asked, interested.

"Oh my yes.A great many times, but you only wondered what made that thought flash through your mind. You never dreamed it was me giving you the thought, to help you clear up some problem that was bothering you," said Aunt Linda.

"We must seem very ungrateful at times," said Helen.

"Not at all," said Helen's father, for we understand your lack of understanding. We would, however, be very happy if you recognized our presence. We have tried very hard at times to either let you see us, or hear our voices, but you have not developed this faculty as well as some others on earth."

"Are you able to make yourself known to some people?" Helen asked. "Oh yes," said Helen's mother, "some people are very receptive." "It is in this way that we can help teach those on earth how to better their world and progress. We will show you more of this, as we take you on different planes while you are here," said Helen's father.

"I should imagine it would be very discouraging to come into our homes and just be ignored," Helen said.

"It is at first, when you try so desperately to comfort those who mourn your leaving the physical body. It causes us a great deal of hurt and sorrow to have them weep over our remains. We try to let them know that we are well and happy and wouldn't want to be back. If we are successful, in getting this thought through to them, we are rewarded by their calm; if not, then we too, suffer emotionally and have our happiness marred," Uncle Frank said.

"I must have caused my share of unhappiness to you folks when you left earth. If I had known, what I know now, I would not have grieved when you left me. As I think back now, I know that at times, you were with me. I remember wondering at the time, if it could be possible, as it seemed that I was so conscious of your presence and little mannerisms I even remember, carrying on a little conversation with you one day. But, afterwards, I decided that I had too vivid an imagination, and that such a thing would be impossible. How that must have hurt you, to think that I could not grasp the fact that you could, and did, come to comfort me."

"We allsuffer in that way, unless those we leave behind understand the true meaning of death," said Uncle Henry.

"The time will come when this condition is bettered for all concerned."

Helen thought she could well understand the hurt they must feel, when they caused so much sorrow to those they loved and had to leave behind, without the understanding of the wonderful life they now led. But, Helen was only to know the full meaning of such helplessness in a short time.

Chapter IV

It was in the midst of their fun and festivities that the first pangs of this hurt came home to Helen.

She was laughing and joking with Uncle Henry, when suddenly Helen stopped her laughing abruptly. She clutched at her breast and let out a gasp.

“Helen, what is it?” her mother asked, knowing too well that Helen had in some way been hurt through someone on earth.

“It’s Paul! I heard him cry out in anguish, my name. He wants me, he needs me, I must go to him. He is frantic. He has found my body and is afraid. He is alone and worried. I must get to him! I must go to him at once and comfort him.

It was the urgent cry they had all heard some time from earth, and knew so well the feeling that had come over Helen.

"Your father and I will go with you, said her mother. Rest assured that we will help him cope with his problem. We can, I am sure, do that."

Before Helen was conscious of traveling, she was by Paul's side. Her desire to be with him, had brought her almost immediately to her own home on earth. He had been like a magnet drawing her back to earth. His voice had left a path of light directing her to his location.

Helen had little inclination now, to question how she had arrived so quickly. Her concern was only for Paul. How selfishly she had been enjoying her new found happiness. Not since first realizing that she had taken leave of her physical body, had she given so much thought to Paul's reactions when he would find her in a coma.

Paul was leaning over her body on the bed and calling out her name.

"Helen! Helen! Can't you hear me?"

Helen went to Paul's side and put her arm around him. "Paul, it's alright. Everything is going to be alright. I'm only in a coma and I'm going to be so much better when this is all over. Don't worry, it's alright."

Paul paid no attention, nor was he conscious of anyone in the room with him. He was still frantically trying to bring her back to consciousness, but now he saw it was no use.

Paul reached for the telephone and called the Doctor. It seemed to relieve him of anxiety while he talked to the Doctor. But while he waited for his arrival, his fears returned again. He paced up and down the floor, not knowing what to do for Helen.

He blamed himself for her condition. He never should have let her stay alone while she was feeling so badly. He had never dreamed a thing like this could happen to her. Why had he been such a blind fool. If he had only known that her condition was this serious; but she had always assured him that all she needed was rest. Now to come home and find her like this ... He paced back and forth, condemning himself.

Helen wished that he would not blame himself. It was not his fault. If he only knew, how it hurt her to hear him reprimanding himself, he would stop. She could hear him. Why couldn't he hear her? Oh if she could only make him hear her and understand that it was alright. She tried over and over again to penetrate her thoughts to him, but with no avail.

Helen spoke to the Doctors from the Heavenly realms who were still working over her body to correct her ills.

"Perhaps you can make him understand" she said.

They shook their heads. "He is too upset emotionally now, to get through to him. We tried to console him before you came."

Helen felt she must do something. She couldn't just stand by and let him carry on so. He had had a terrible shock, coming home to find her like this.

Helen realized now selfishly she had been enjoying herself. She hadn't stopped to think what a shock it would be for Paul. She had been so engrossed in her new surroundings and new found interests, that this part of it had faded from her thoughts. Strange how completely she had left all earth problems behind her.

Now, more than anything, she wanted to comfort Paul. She wanted above all else to let him know she was alright; but she couldn't seem to manage.

Helen was beginning to understand, through experience, the great hurt that death brought. To those who left their earthly bodies, there was but one regret; to comfort and bring understanding to the loved ones they left behind. She felt torn and hurt by Paul's grief. The only penalty of death, she thought. If she could tell him that she was alright, they would both be much happier. If he understood how much he was hurting her by his compassion, he would not take on so.

Helen vowed that when she returned to her body, to live on earth again, she would tell Paul of her experience. She would make him see death through her eyes. And make him understand that grieving for those who die, only cause them heartache and a feeling of helplessness.

Helen reached out and put her arm around her husband. She hoped to comfort him and in some way destroy his fears that were causing them both so much sorrow. When all her efforts failed, she burst into tears. Her mother and father comforted her. They understood just what she felt in her heart, for they too had gone through this when their time of departure from earth had come.

Helen, herself, had caused them great sorrow by her lack of understanding. She had been so young to leave, and had been overcome with grief. It was all very natural, the hurt and sorrow she had felt, but still that didn't lessen the sympathy they felt for her. They too, had felt helpless to comfort her when she had wept and called out in desperation for them to come back and not leave her. Her longing for them had only caused them sorrow. In time the great torture of her sorrowing had lessened, and she had gone on with life. It was not until she had adjusted herself to her life without them, that they had been able to find complete happiness in their new world.

In the many years that Helen's parents had been gone from earth, they had learned more and more the need for a better understanding of death by those who still lived on earth. If they could learn to understand that they lived a happy and full life beyond the grave, in a world of God's designing, perhaps they too, would rejoice instead of sorrowing. Death is inevitable; yet people on earth have not learned to cope with it. Death and birth are as natural as the coming of spring flowers after the winter has passed. Death, if people realized it, is like the coming of spring. The physical body is shed like the winter's gloom, leaving the soul free and unhampered to enjoy the beginning of a new life. Where there is no gloom of winter, to be dispelled, before the soul can unfold and grow in their new life. Still people sorrow over this wonderful adventure that is given to those they love.

It is strange too, for if someone we care for has the opportunity to make a journey into some beautiful but strange land on earth, we help him prepare for that journey. We speed him on his way with good wishes and a smile. We will miss him of course, but we are glad that he is able to see the places that we have never seen. We do not then grieve for him, but look forward to the messages he may send us, telling us of the life that he has learned of in this far off place.

Death should be thought of in the same way. We travel on our way, seeing a new and beautiful world, and are anxious to send messages home so that those who are not so fortunate, may glimpse the beauties of our world through our tales.

The door between the two worlds could stand wide open, if those on the earth would heed our messages and believe them as they do those they receive by letter. Our communication system is so much more direct and personal. We come to tell our experiences in person. If people would let down the barrier it would all seem so simple and lend more happiness to all. The time will come for more than just a few, to have direct contact with those we have left on earth. Then this needless sorrowing for those taken from earth will no longer tear at the hearts of either.

Helen's mother was interrupted in thought, by the sound of Paul's voice.

"Helen is breathing, she is still alive. I wish the doctor would get here. She lies so motionless. Still someway, it seems to me she is not lying there at all, but moving about the room as usual. Strange I feel that way; but I'm so worried it's a wonder I'm in my right mind."

Helen crossed the room again to Paul's side and put her hand on his shoulder. He turned as if half expecting someone to be there. Helen had hopes, perhaps now she would have some success.

"I thought sure someone came into this room", he said aloud. "I thought for a minute it might be the Doctor. I must be getting jittery. Why doesn't he get here? He must get here before it is too late."

At that moment someone came in the front door.

Paul called out, "Doctor, is that you? Come right on up. I can't seem to bring Helen to. She just lies there, and won't answer me. What can be the matter with her?"

The Doctor bent over Helen's body and rolled her eyelids back with his fingers. He then took her pulse and blood pressure.

"She is in a coma," he said, "That is why you couldn't rouse her. I would like to take her to the hospital where we can make a more thorough check. She will need constant watching, and I believe the hospital is the place for her. It will do no harm to move her, and if it is alright with you, I will call an ambulance."

"Whatever you think is best," Paul said. "The main thing is for her to get well. I can't stand to see her like that."

Paul paced back and forth while the doctor called the ambulance. "What could have brought this on so suddenly?" Paul asked. "Is she in grave danger?"

"Many things could cause a coma of this kind. It could be a pressure on a nerve, or perhaps a hemorrage, causing a stroke. I would want to make a more thorough examination before making a complete diagnosis. That is why I want her in the hospital where we have everything at our disposal. Have you any idea when this happened?"

"No, I found her just like this when I cam home this evening.

I called you just as soon as I realized something was wrong. Usually she lies down around three o'clock for awhile. Evidently, she had done just that. I am thankful that it didn't happen while she was coming up the stairs. Heavens, what a fool I have been to leave her alone!"

"Now then Paul, don't blame yourself. If anyone is to blame for her being alone when this happened, it is myself. I certainly never dreamed this would happen, or I would have suggested that someone be with her at all times. No, it is just one of those things that are unpredictable. I think she will pull out of this, so do not worry too much. She seemed so much improved last week when she visited my office. This, however, may prove to be for the best. Often times a thing of this kind is a climax to a condition such as she had, and removes completely the cause of all her trouble. Let us hope, this will be true in her case."

It was a strange experience for Helen to stand there and hear herself discussed. She went over to the Doctors from the world she was visiting, and asked them their opinion. They smiled at her and assured her that all was working out very well.

"There is a lot of truth in what that Doctor of yours was telling your husband," one of them told her. "If this had not developed, you might have suffered along, for some time, without gaining much. Now the cause will be removed, and you will once more feel well in your physical body. That was what you wanted, wasn't it?"

Helen smiled at him and thanked him for the reassurance.

Helen and her parents went with them to the hospital.

She didn't feel of much help to Paul, but she wanted to stay with him.

She wanted desperately to give him a thought of encouragement. He seemed somewhat relieved after they reached the hospital and had talked matters over with the Doctor. He was much calmer now. Perhaps she would be able to help him obtain a better attitude, regarding her condition.

Her father said that he thought the three of them could accomplish this now. They gathered around Paul as he sat by the bedside. His mind seemed to be relaxed now. It would be much easier to penetrate his mind with their thoughts while he was quieted down. Before, he had been so upset by his own mind thrashing around with the problem; now, he seemed less upset.

Helen wondered what to tell him. She didn't want to cause him any confusion. He didn't realize that she was out of her body and she must not plant the thought of her dying in his mind. Making him feel her presence would only upset him. Perhaps it would be better if she just talked to him as she always did when he was upset and worried. Yes, that would be the best way to comfort him. She stood very close to him and began to talk.

"Do not worry, darling. Things are never as black as they look. Remember all the times you have worried when there was no need to, all that worry for nothing. Helen will be so much better when this is all over that you will be glad that it had happened. The Doctor spoke of that possibility himself. Think of how nice it will be then and do not think of this moment. When one is in a coma, they feel no pain, so she is not suffering. Why do you upset yourself? That does not help her any. She is resting. Why don't you rest?

She would want you to rest. In a few days she will be all well again, and you will want to feel well enough then, to sit here with her. Why don't you go and eat your dinner. You can't make her better by sitting here in this room with her. The nurse will be here soon to care for her. You will only be in the way. Helen wouldn't want you to sit here all night, you know that."

Helen paused for a moment. Had she penetrated her thoughts to him. He had seemed to be listening intently. Now, he rose from the chair beside the bed, and leaned over her body. Yes, he seemed more relieved now. He was now thinking of the truth that she had just told him, and going over it in his mind. It seemed to him the logical thing to do. He seemed to have things straightened out now, and was thinking more clearly and sensibly.

"I did it! He heard me! Helen said joyfully. He doesn't realize it was my words going through his mind, but I don't care as long as I got results. He thinks that he thought it out himself. Yet he should know that he was listening to some one talk. This is really a wonderful thing, once you get on to it. More people should make use of it."

The nurse came into the room and said, "I will be with Mrs. Terry all night. The day nurse will relieve me in the morning, so she will have someone with her constantly. You look tired, why don't you go home. There is nothing you can do tonight. It is doubtful she will rally through the night. I promise to call you the minute she rallies, if that will make you feel easier."

Paul hesitated, and then said, "Yes, you do that. I guess I wouldn't be of any help here, probably only in the way."

Helen was very happy to hear Paul's decision. She knew

that her thoughts had relieved him. He had his feet back on the ground now, and had a hold of himself.

As he left the hospital, Helen and her parents were close by his side. They sat with him while he ate his dinner, and later, with him at home. When he was finally asleep for the night, Helen and her parents left him, feeling quite pleased with their success.

They rejoined the relatives who were awaiting their return from earth. Helen was quite elated as she told them of her success with thought projection.

"I certainly am glad that you explained it to me, before the occasion came up for us to use it. I little thought at the time, that it would serve me so well, in quite such a short time. I thought of it then, more as a game. Now I understand fully, the real purpose and need for such a phenomena."

"You are only beginning to know the real value of such a feat," said Uncle Henry. Wait until you actually see with your own eyes the great things that are accomplished by this method. Then you will be truly astounded. You have no idea of the things that we are going to show you during your visit. We have things, we each must do, so we will leave you now; but will see you tomorrow." After she had bid them all goodbye, she wondered what Uncle Henry had meant, by saying they all had things to do. Certainly, it didn't seem to her, that there was anything very important to do. Besides, it was late. At least, it was night on earth, but Helen realized now that it was not night where they were. She had been thinking of Paul when they returned, and not noticed until now.

"Doesn't it get night over here?" she asked.

"Well," said her father, "if you mean dark, No ... But I suppose you might call it night. We give little thought to time. Time is not tabulated here, as it is on earth. We have certain periods when we do certain things, but we do not calculate in terms of time, as they do on earth. Days, nights, weeks or years, are not of so much importance to us. Time is no factor to us, in the sense that it is to earth people. We go about our work unhurried."

"Then why did the folks say that they had things to do, now?" Helen asked, eager to know where they had gone.

"We all do things at different periods of the day or night. We each have a routine of our own. Of course it varies from time to time, just as people on earth, do different things in different periods of their life. We do pretty much the things we like to do, and are best fitted for. Sometimes we attend lectures, so that we may learn, from the great intellectuals of the higher planes, how to best fit ourselves to do the most good. Sometimes we, ourselves, go to lower planes to teach them what we have learned, so that they may be better able to progress. Others, go to earth, to watch over those still living there. No one in the physical body is ever alone. They are constantly attended by someone from this side whose work it is to guard over them. Then of course, we have periods of recreation, doing whatever we like to do. I do not just know, right now, what each of your relatives are doing for their particular work. But, they each have a specific work to do each day. When I am busy, I do not see them all the time, anymore than you keep in close contact with what your friends are doing from day to day. If I am inclined to see them or know of their whereabouts, I can do so and find out just what line of work they are doing. Would you like to have me find out just what each of them is doing now?" Helen's mother asked.

"No, I was only curious to know why they had to leave," Helen said. "But don't you get tired, and need rest?"

"We do not get tired as earth people do; not physically tired. Perhaps you would call it emotional tiredness, or mental fatigue. But it is an entirely different thing than earth people ever experience. We do not require sleep, nor rest of that kind. Our souls need to be renewed by Divine strength. We are in that way restored mentally and spiritually as our needs are felt. Sometimes we sit quietly and ask for wisdom from God's great storehouse. Other times we go to the Cathedral and listen to inspiritional music which leaves our souls soothed. You have had a trying emotional strain, perhaps you would like to experience this for yourself," said Helen's father.,

"Yes I would," said Helen, "if I am not keeping you from something you should be doing."

"Our only work for the next few days is to be with you and show you this world. We hope to show you many interesting things and explain them to you as best we can. Some of it will be beyond your power to comprehend, as you are too inexperienced to grasp it fully. However, it will be of great interest to you," said Helen's mother.

"May I explore your house before we go to the Cathedral?" Helen asked.

"Why child, haven't you been taken through the house yet?" Helen's father asked, taking her by the arm and escorting her around.

Helen didn't miss a thing. It was 'like going through any new house, looking for new and unusual things. However, it was the commonplace things that she was so accustomed to on earth, that amazed her the most.

Opening a door and finding it to be a closet, she said, "Why mother! You have clothes closets just as we have on earth!"

"Why of course. What did you expect?" her mother said, laughing at her daughter's surprise.

"Well, it's just that I had not stopped to think about clothing before. Where do you get your clothing? There doesn't seem to be any stores where you can buy them; at least I didn't see any.

"Well dear, I might ask you where you got your clothing. You did not bring your material clothing with you, you know. You are wearing spiritual clothes yourself," said Helen's mother with a twinkle in her eye.

Helen glanced down at herself, and then looked rather sheepishly for a moment. Then burst into laughter. "That's a good one on me," she said. "Here I am asking you where you get your clothing, and I don't know how I got mine. Fact was, I hadn't realized before that I wasn't dressed in my usual clothes. But I always knew, that whatever happened to people when they left earth life, that they did not take their earthly possessions with them. Perhaps I thought that I was an exception," she laughed.

"You are not alone in your realization. Many people do not realize for some time after they are here, that they are wearing spiritual clothes. Fact is, many of them will not believe when told, that they no longer have their physical body. They insist, that they are not dead. Sometimes it is quite a problem to make them understand that they have made the change of death. It is only through their own experience, as time goes on, that they are convinced. Sometimes it is quite amusing to hear their arguments," Helen's mother related.

"In your case," said Helen's father, "you were not so hard to convince, that the clothing you are now wearing is not the same as you had while on earth. Now then, how you came by them was purely a matter of need; and so they were provided for you.

Even over here, we do like to be clothed. All our needs are provided for us in very much the same manner, through Divine power. We have what we need, and as much as we need. We have several different changes of clothing which lasts for a certain period of time. However, they do wear out, so to speak. The substance they are made of, is only lasting for a certain length of time. When that time is up, we are given replacements. We have our likes in colors and cut, and are given accordingly. To a certain extent, we must be deserving, to have our choice of colors and variations of material."

"Will I have others, while I am here too?" asked Helen.

"Most certainly; they will be supplied for you as you require them," Helen's mother replied.

This was all most interesting to Helen. She closed the closet door that held her mother's various garments and went on through the house.

"Who washed the dishes and cleared things away? You would never know that you had entertained guests, everything is so clean. When I have company for dinner, my house looks a mess when they go home," Helen said.

"You are, a question box," said Helen's father, delighted to have the opportunity to enlighten his daughter. "But it is only natural for you to be so inquisitive; as we all are, when we first come here. But some things are pretty difficult to explain. You will just have to accept what we tell you for a fact. It takes some time of study to understand fully the Powers that move in this world. All things here and on earth are created and taken away by this power. A power of unlimited force. It is necessary to learn in this world that this Power of God is eternal and everlasting. It rules our every movement and the life that surrounds us. His laws, predominate and govern this world of spirit. The first law of this land, is that there shall be no disorder allowed to remain. Therefore, when things become disrupted and unsightly, they are removed from existence. Nothing is wasted, but removed from where it is no longer needed. Thus God works in his mysterious ways in Heaven, as on earth. Thus the dishes and leftover food, no more of use to us, was taken back, through this power, to the great storehouse of God. Is that at all clear to you?"

"Well, not exactly clear," said Helen, "but a lot of things that I have experienced myself, are not really easy to understand. Yet I know they are true and existing, so I will accept things as true, that you tell me.

"I can feel this Power that you speak of so often, but I am still a little baffled by it. It's in the air and touches you wherever you are, but it is hard to explain even to one's self. One knows so well of its existence, and so readily accepts it when he is here where he can feel it and see the wonderful things it bestows. Living here and seeing things with one's own eyes, it does not seem so strange that these things can be and are done. We do not question on earth, when a newborn baby arrives, where the power of life comes from. If we delved into this question, we undoubtedly would become more baffled than we are. For we already know, that a body of flesh and blood cannot live and breathe without the soul, or spark of life given from God's storehouse. Man can create the physical body through scientific experiments; but all such efforts to produce a living body, have failed. Yes, father, we must all admit, whether we live on earth or in Heaven, that this power exists, and must be acknowledged by all who claim to be intelligent. Life and death are the miracles of Earth, and the only, truly great things that Earth has to compare with all the wonders I find over here.

"Heaven and Earth are so very much alike in outline. We have the same things on Earth as you have here. Trees, flowers, grass, sky, buildings, homes, churches, and people, all the same things; but oh so different. It is like comparing a finely cut diamond with a piece of clay. It might be the same size and form; but in reality there is no comparison. The beauty, sparkle, and life of the diamond, is like your world over here. While Earth in comparison seems now, more like clay. It seems drab and lifeless, after seeing the beauties and wonderful things in this world. Yet, they are so very much alike. Strange, how two places can seem so very much alike; and still be so vastly different. It is something you feel, rather than see with your eyes. At first, this escaped me; but now I can see, that Earth with all its progress, is still like an unpolished stone."

"Yes, and you have not begun to scratch the surface, in the short time you have been here. Nor will you, by the time you return to Earth. It is ever unfolding to those who live here. We constantly find new fields to enter as we progress and learn. We are ever eager to gain more knowledge from those who have progressed ahead of us, so that we too, may enjoy the advanced phenomanas of the higher realms.

"But come, you will never see these things for yourself if we stay here," said Helen's father, pleased by his daughter's interest.

Chapter V.

They entered the Cathedral and made their way to the pew.

Helen was lost to those around her by her intense feeling of awe. She seated herself slowly, as she looked all around this place of solace. Its atmosphere was one of beauty and calm, and held her spellbound. She felt that she had been lifted into still another new world. The feeling that stole over her filled her with reverence and peace.

Organ music pealed forth in tones so soft and mellow that Helen relaxed completely. She felt as though she were in a dream and drifting on a peaceful ocean. Her soul felt like the warm rays of sunlight were flooding over her. All thoughts that had held her interest were now removed. She was neither curious nor conscious of those about her. She sat in complete silence, as did others who had gathered for this time of solace. Helen was at peace as she had never been before.

Suddenly in the quiet of the room a voice spoke, and as it did, a flood of beautiful rays filled the room. It was more beautiful than any rainbow that Helen had ever seen.

She sat completely spellbound by this glorious demonstration. The voice that was speaking did not seem to be in their midst. It came from nowhere. Helen listened.

"Let your souls be filled with the love of God. His ever radiant love will give you peace and will restore your souls. His presence, you all feel. Drink and be refreshed by his love. It is ever yours for the seeking, and His power will strengthen the weak. Let all who seek this hour of solace, be filled with inspiration, that each may know the true power that lies within his soul. God sees fit to direct your path into the ways you must rightfully go. Shed all cares and be restored through his love."

These words were spoken softly and with reverence and beauty.

Helen sat motionless and relaxed, looking in the direction the voice had sounded. There seemed to be no one accompanying, by presence, this voice.

Then as clearly as the voice itself, there appeared the person who had spoken. This was truly the greatest pleasure of all for Helen, for there before her, stood Jesus, radiant and calm. He was the most beautiful spirit that she had seen. Different from all the others; but only because of his great radiance. His countenance was like a flood light, throwing out bright rays. His smile was tender and filled with love of all humanity.

Jesus had come to bring this message of love from the realms on high, that they might go from this house of God, inspired by his love.

As he stood there before them, now so that all might see him, he bade them to listen and heed the voice of God as He directed and counseled their souls.

"In this hour of communing with God, your soul will be filled with wisdom. Let not your hearts be troubled, for God is always with you. You feel His presence, and are filled with His will. Go your way, doing your work, for then the glories of God will unfold before you. The way is ever open for your progression. Let nothing hold you from reaching out for more truth and knowledge. Your souls know no bounds and therefore there is no limit to your progression. Seek and you shall find, the wisdom to open the way to that which you desire!"

Upon completion of this message, Jesus went as he had come. Back into his own realm.

The music again, was soft and mellow. Whence it came, Helen did not know. There was no organ in sight, nor hands that played. It drifted through the Cathedral with melodious vibrations. It penetrated the room with all its beautiful chords, filling the quiet room with serenity.

Helen once more listened to the music that was so beautiful and felt a flood of renewed strength pouring through her. All fear and restraint was taken from her as she listened. She seemed filled with understanding and love, of this beautiful land that she was so privileged to glimpse. She felt inspired to learn more of this great wisdom that had purged her soul and left her so refreshed.

Helen's father touched her on the arm and mentioned they were leaving.

Once outside the Cathedral, Helen took a deep breath and sighed. "It is the most wonderful thing that I have ever experienced. There are no words to describe it. It is beautiful ... Serene .... uplifting.. and peaceful. I didn't realize I was in need of rest, as I didn't recognize that sort of fatigue. The excitement of being here, and my episode with Paul, was a strain emotionally. I can see that now."

"I thought that it would rest you," said her mother. We often feel the need for relaxation."

"Yes, and it was a wonderful experience for you," said her father. "We never could have told you in words, it has to be felt."

Helen still felt the beauty of it and it was hard to throw it off. It lingered in her very being. Not that she wanted to be rid of this new sensation, but its presence filled one so completely with a sense of the overwhelming power, that was so capable of these manifestations. Seeing Jesus and hearing him speak, filled her with new thoughts.

"Does Jesus often come to the Cathedral as he did today?" Helen asked.

"Jesus goes wherever he is needed. Sometimes he comes to the Cathedral as he did today; other times he appears to those who come from earth and feel his need. Jesus has progressed far, and is a wise teacher. His duties are many and varied," said Helen's mother.

"But I supposed that Jesus stayed with God and was too supreme a soul to still have to help other souls. I thought that he would be more privileged than others,"Helen said, rather dismayed.

"Jesus was a privileged man while he lived on earth too," said Helen's father. "He knew the things that we are only learning now. He had the wisdom endowed him by God, but he was ever humble in his mission. He knew then, as he knows now, the privilege of serving humanity. He hasn't changed in this way, any more than the rest of us change, as to the type of person we are. He is only continuing his work that he started on earth. It is only natural for him to preach God's teachings and help those who seek truth. He still serves God in his many ways. But he too, now is unhampered by earth's surroundings."

"But Jesus was the son of God, sent to earth from His storehouse of souls to fill a purpose. Jesus was a man of flesh and blood, born of earthly woman, to teach the earth people of a life existing after death. He was as you and I; but with a wisdom far greater than men of his time. He was fortunate in realizing his earthly mission and carrying on in face of many obstacles. He was attuned to the guidance of his Heavenly father and was guided accordingly.

"Other men, since that time, too, have been sent to earth on a special mission. It is not always to teach a religious truth. That happened to be the mission of Jesus; but others are sent to bring other things of benefit to the earth people. Think of the great inventors. They are also servants of God, inspired to bring things into being for the improvement and progress of the world. They are just as much the son of God, and doing his work on earth by fulfilling their mission, as was Jesus. But perhaps you will see how true this is, by actually seeing it in process. All things are originated here and then given to earth as we will show you later," Helen's father explained.

"We on earth do not think of it that way," said Helen. But as you tell it, it seems very logical and true. All of us can not be great, and do a great work, but I suppose each in his own way does something of purpose. We all are a cog in the wheel of earth, each doing our little share to make it a better place. Some of us do not live up to our trust; and I suppose that is why the world is in the condition that it is."

Helen's father laughed at his daughter. She certainly was taking the whole thing very seriously. "You can laugh at me if you want to. But after all I never realized before just how serious living was. I probably haven't accomplished the things that I was sent to Earth to do. I supposed, that we were just to live along each day, doing whatever came our way. But this makes it have a main purpose for our existence on Earth. Gee ... I can't think of anything that I have contributed to the world. When I get back I guess I'll have to change may ways."

Helen's father roared with laughter. "Why child," he said between chuckles, "You have only started to live. You have been growing up and gaining knowledge from Earth's surroundings. Earth is your kindergarten, and it is there, that you prepare yourself for this life. You must have earth experiences to be ready to live here. Your childhood is a play time, during which time you are absorbing many of life's lessons. You are only now, ready to do your part on earth. "But," he laughed, "do not get the idea that you must do something great and outstanding in order to fill your mission in life. No, many of us, as you so aptly put it, are cogs in the wheel of life, adding in some small measure to the completion of the pattern, set for earth. You just go back and be your own sweet self, and I am sure that you will do much good. You have already proven to be an important cog in the wheel of life."

Helen looked pleased and surprised. "I have!" she said,

beaming. "Why of course," said her mother. "We each, in our own little way, contribute something worthwhile, although at the time we do not realize its value. Some gesture of kindness, or a little deed performed, without realizing its true value. These are the important things in life. Not the big things we do for acclaim; but the little thoughtful things we do in our everyday life that add a bit of joy. These are the things that make life worthwhile. So you see, why your father said that you shared in making the world a better place. When you return to earth, just keep on being joyful and brightening up the world. Laughter and joy are needed just as badly, as are things of material worth. People are too apt to stress the big things, and forget the importance of little things. Always remember that."

"Then life is really simple, after all," said Helen. it is really a matter of living each day to the best of our ability, doing in our small way whatever lies on our path."

"That's right," said Helen's father. Do the best you can under the circumstances, and it will surprise you, the stride you make."

"Where are we going now?" said Helen, as she noticed the strangeness of her surroundings.

"We thought we would show you some of the lower planes. Would you like that?" her father asked.

"Oh yes! It may make me strive harder for a higher goal." Helen laughed, as she made this remark; but she was half serious.

Chapter VI

As they walked along, Helen watched the many people they came in contact with. Everyone seemed to be doing something that held their attention. They all seemed very happy and contented with their active life.

They were passing through the plane on which her parents lived, but there did seem to be some difference in the different territories. It was quite like passing through a State on Earth. Helen remarked about this to her parents.

"That's exactly what it is like," said her father. This plane is made up of varied people and interests. Therefore, there must be various accommodations. All people in a city or state, do not have the same taste in things. Their likes and dislikes influence their surroundings. You will notice along here the difference in the building construction. It is of a different design than where your mother and I live. That is because these people prefer this type of architecture.

"We will pass through sections where certain nationalities are found. This is not because of any discrimination, nor mean that they are on a lower or higher plane. This is the same plane that we live on, only another section. It is only natural that people of a kind, are happier with their own people. They have certain customs that they enjoy, and go on with, after coming to live here. They would not find their Heaven, unless they were permitted to abide in the surroundings that they are accustomed, any more than we would. We will, if there is time, take you to visit some of the different races while you are here."

"Now we will leave our plane and go directly to the lowest plane and work up," said Helen's mother. "This plane will be very interesting to you, but not very uplifting. You will notice a drabness that exists on no other plane. But remember the people who live on the lowest plane are those who have committed some great wrong, and thus have not desired to better themselves. It will not be such a pleasure trip, but will enlighten you on many things we could not tell you. In reality I suppose it would be what earth people call Hell. But we have no Hell created by God. The conditions existing on the lowest plane are caused only by those who live there. They can, if they desire, better their ways of living. This is the problem. Many of them neither care to, nor can be filled with the desire. You will see what I mean when you see the attitude they take."

"Here we are," said Helen's father. "This is the lowest plane."

Helen looked about her. She didn't say anything for a moment. There was a drabness. No beauty that she had found on the other plane that she had visited. It was almost like a fog hovering over this plane. The air seemed dense and clouded. It was ugly after the beauty of the plane where her parents lived. How could anyone wish to remain there, when they could so easily work up to the other planes. Her father had told her they need not stay here, and had been told of the beauty of the other planes. Why then, did they not take advantage of their opportunity.

They walked along among the people. They themselves, cast a cloud about them. The other souls that Helen had contacted seemed radiant. It was like being with a happy carefree child and then having a sulky naughty child given to you in its place. The atmosphere was heavy with sullenness. It was like being with a mean hateful person that filled the surroundings with an atmosphere of gloom. Helen had encountered people on Earth who had filled her with a feeling of gloom. Many times she had tried to cheer a gloomy sullen person up, but could not penetrate the wall of comdemnation, that they had built around themselves. Helen could see as she looked about, what a task it would be to help these poor souls. They didn't want to be helped. They were happy in their unhappiness. What could one do to make them see the light.

There were many people there from the other planes. Helen could tell the difference at sight. They were the souls that radiated beauty. She watched them milling around with these people of the low plane. They were trying to help them better themselves, but Helen could see that their efforts were most in vain.

"Let's stop here," said Helen's mother. "This little lady seems willing to be shown the way. Perhaps we can help her. She is beginning to be desirous of a better life. She is throwing out thoughts that she now sees the errors of her way.

They paused at the side of the woman, who sat rocking back and forth on the stoop of her dingy home. It was a home of her own making, for she in her soul had been crude and uncouth.

While on earth this woman had gloried in the fact that she was mean and hateful. Delighted in hurting others, intentionally. Planned coldly, deeds of unkindness, knowing well the wrong she was committing, but ever going on. Her thoughts were as black as her deeds, and she had not one kind generous thought or deed to her credit. If she had tried to do her best under bad circumstances, she would not have found herself on this plane after death. She had been conscious of her meanness and knew the wrong she was doing, but had put forth special effort to do worse.

At first when she was very young, she had started on a small scale by committing harm to living things. Instead of repenting as most children do when told of their wrongs, she tried to become worse. As years went on and she saw the meanness that she had developed, she only laughed at the blackness of her sins. She had defied every law of human-ness, doing unjust deeds throughout her entire life. Little things at first and then big things. Her soul was black and unrepenting.

Helen asked her father if all souls were equally as good, when sent to earth. "Or are some souls endowed with these traits that give them an unfair chance?"

"When a soul leaves the storehouse of God, it is pure and untarnished," he said. "Each soul grows into whatever he makes of himself. We each are given the same instincts of right and wrong. How we adjust ourselves to life and its temptations, is up to each of us. We are alone, responsible for our soul," he said.

"But there must be some good in each of these people," Helen said.

"The people on this plane are more bad than good, otherwise they wouldn't be here, they would be on one of the other planes. All of us do bad things during our life time. It is what we do, and how we do it, and under what circumstances, that count. it is more the motive behind the deed, than the deed itself. Many of us commit wrongs without intentionally doing so, and this is taken into consideration. Again, it is the thought behind our actions, more than the action itself. If we are conscientiously living to the best of our ability and understanding, then we are doing the best that we are capable of doing. But the thing that counts here and on earth is the willingness on our part to right our wrongs. This is the thing that holds these people from from progression and a happier life; they do not wish to be better," Helen's father explained.

Helen's mother had been talking to the little lady on the stoop, and now Helen and her father joined her.

Helen's mother was saying, "If you could only see the other planes that you could be living on. It would be like going from rags to riches. Certainly now, after all this time, you must be ready to leave this plane. You must be filled with this desire after being told of your possibilities. Won't you let me help you to accomplish this?"

The little lady had stared at her without expression or gratitude, but now made an effort at a wane smile.

"I have been told of these planes before and can't get

interested," she said. "What's the matter with this plane? Don't you like it? I'm quite happy here. I fit here. Yes, I guess I belong here with my own kind. I am as I am, and will never be any different. I'm me and you're you, and the two of us would never fit in together. Besides I can be my own ugly self here. If I went to your plane I would have to be good, and I'm afraid it ain't in me. Old Liza, will always be the same. I've been over here several years now and no one has been able to change me."

"Is it because you think you would not fit in? If that is the reason, you have nothing to fear. For until you were ready to fit in, you would not leave here. By the time that you are prepared to leave here, you would be put with people of your own standing. So you see, you would feel just as much at home in the other planes as you do here. Each time that you make progression, you would outgrow your other surroundings," Helen's mother explained patiently.

"You mean to say, that if I did try; now I'm just supposing, that I wouldn't be looked down on?"

"Why should you be? You would deserve what ever you had. You would have worked and earned the right to the pleasures that would be yours. No! Of course you wouldn't be looked down on."

"Well it's too much effort anyway. I've got too much to right," said Liza. "It would take too long, and, after all, I'm alright here."

"Well eternity, is a long time," said Helen's mother. I should think that the sooner you begin to right these wrongs, the better."

"Eternity..." Liza mumbled. "Eternity ... hummm. Eternity,

huh? I never thought of that. She glanced around her and smirked. "A pretty picture!"

Then she jerked herself up haughtily, peered around Helen's mother, and said, "Who's that girl? She must be fresh from earth with that darn life cord dangling from her." Earth! That's as bad a place as this."

"This is our daughter Helen," said her mother.

Helen stepped forth and extended her hand to Liza. She smiled at her, and wished that in some way she could help the poor soul.

"Well what do you think of this plane?" she asked Helen, nastily. S'pose you don't like it either. No, s'pose you don't. For the first time Liza seemed a bit ashamed of her surroundings. Then she said, "Well see to it that you don't end up here. Let me serve as a lesson to you. I'm as good a lesson as you will ever see. I could have been just as good as your folks here. Oh yes I could!.. Only I didn't want to be; I wanted to be, bad. Well, I was. And now look at me! Go ahead! Look at me! Oh, what difference does it make? I'm sorry .. sorry I blew off like that."

Helen said, "Why that's alright. We all get upset at times."

"At times!" said Liza, "I guess I'm always that way."

"By the way, what are you doing over here?" Liza asked Helen. "I'm on a visit, while my body is recovering from an illness. My body is in a coma."

"I was in a coma one time, and I didn't go a visiting the

high Heavens," she said. "How come?"

"I guess I am one of the few lucky ones," said Helen.

"You mean you are probably more deserving than I was," said Liza. "And, you probably are. I haven't even seen Heaven, yet.'

"You could though, if you wanted to," said Helen, sweetly.

" I s'pose" said Liza .

"Why don't you want to?" asked Helen. "I think it would be nice. I am sure you would be glad if you tried."

"Oh do you? Well I'm not trying. I like it here. It's my place," said Liza, not very convincingly.

"Oh I am sure you would like it if you saw it!" said Helen, eager to tell her of its beauties.

"Is it really as nice as they say it is?" asked Liza hopefully.

"Oh yes! Isn't it, mother?"

"Yes, and I am sure you would think so too, Liza. Why not see for yourself?" Helen's mother asked encouragingly.

"Oh yes, please do!" said Helen. "Then when I come over to stay, you can tell me what, you, think of it. I will be thinking of your progress and wondering how much headway you have made. Why don't you do it, Liza? Just to surprise me. Oh I think it would be wonderful if you would. You have no idea how really nice it is!"

"Well don't get so excited; or the first thing you know, I will get the crazy notion that I could do it," said Liza, looking more interested than she had at any time.

"Why of course you could do it. You said you did a good job of being bad. Well you could do just as much with that will, at doing good, couldn't you?" Helen asked, trying to tease her into it.

"S'pose I could. If I set my mind to it just as hard," said Liza, mischievously.

The challenge that Helen had made, brought response as no other inducement had.

"I'll tell you what I'll do," said Liza. "I'll be there to greet you when you come over next time. It will be sort of a race between us, who comes out on top. I got a lot of catching up to do, but I'll wager that I'll at least progress far enough by that time, to be able to be on hand to greet you. But you better do your best to live a while and give me a fair chance. Yes sir! I'll bet I'll win that wager too," Liza said, grinning from ear to ear.

"Well you know I'm not going to be idle all that time," said Helen, laughing. I'll try to keep up with you. And if I am any judge of your power, once you set your mind to a thing, I will have to live a pretty worthwhile life. But it's a bet! It will keep us both on our toes."

"You bet it will, young lady! For when Liza makes up her mind to do a thing, whether good or bad, she does it with her greatest all. How do I go about starting," she asked

Helen's mother.

"You are already started," said Helen's mother. "The very decision to do it, has started you on your way. Don't you feel better already?"

"Well I don't feel so mean and hateful, if that is what you mean?" Liza said, laughing and happiness shining from her face. "Yes, I guess I do feel better. Sort of lifted up out of my sallowness. I sure am anxious to see some progress though, now that my mind's made up. Now I can't wait to earn the right to get out of this place. Confidentially, I never did really like it, but was too darn stubborn to even admit it to myself. How any one person, can be so pig-headed and set in their miserable way, is almost unbelievable. I am truly grateful to you, my girl, for that challenge. Nothing else under God's sun could have made me want to change. Go along now, and see the rest of these self satisfied souls, that don't know enough to take the advantage of what is offered. Who knows, some day, I might be back here trying to pound some sense into them," Liza said, beaming at the prospect.

Helen's mother leaned over and whispered in Liza's ear, "Maybe by telling some of your friends that you are going to leave here, you can persuade them to do likewise. That in itself, would be a good deed and start you on your way. See what success you have. You might surprise yourself."

"Say! I'll do that. I'll bet I could get at least ten to work along with me. Sort of a contest between us," Liza said, tickled over the suggestion. Go along now. Don't hamper me in my work," she said, like a happy child with a new toy, eager to get started at the game.

It was difficult to tell who was the happier over the turn of events. Helen and her family were greatly pleased over Liza's change of heart; but Liza was a new person. Her excitement and happiness was plain to see by all who witnessed. And now she didn't care who saw the change that came over her. Now that she had been awakened by this spark of determination to right her wrongs, nothing was going to stand in her way.

Liza was like that. Once she set her mind to a thing nothing stopped her. She only had to be convinced that she wanted to do a thing, and it was just as well as done. It had been this same will, that had kept her from being helped by anyone before. She had made up her mind that if she had lived a bad life on earth, she would continue the same. She always felt that one could do just as good a job at being bad as at anything else. And she had spent so much of her time being bad, she saw no reason for changing her ways. She could have done that on earth; she didn't have to die in order to have that opportunity. No, until today, she had never had the desire to make amends. But, once she saw a purpose in it, she was determined to do a good job. She would work and work, and reach the highest goal possible. Nothing would be too great an obstacle to overcome. That was the way Liza was.

Helen saw all types of people on her visit to this low plane. Some, hardened criminals that had no regrets. Others, who like Liza, had lived selfishly. Only Liza, was bad and admitted it, during her earth life. While some of these people, had lived on the surface, as upright christian people; but in their soul they had been as black with sin. These were the hypocrites who condemned others, while they themselves, lived in "glass houses." They had succeeded on earth in fooling their fellowmen; but their souls had become weak and sordid.

Helen walked along with her parents, noticing the vast difference in this surrounding. Besides the cloudiness that seemed to hover this plane, there were other differences. True, that there was on this plane the same lay-out as on the plane where her parents lived; but it was like comparing day and night. Here, there was not the beauty that had filled Helen with so much delight. The homes and buildings were commonplace. The flowers did not seem able to flourish in such full beauty on this plane. Helen noticed all these things, and remarked about it to her parents. "It seems so drab and dingy here," said Helen. This plane seems to have all the characteristics of the people who live here."

"That is why this plane is known as the dark plane," said Helen's father. "The people who live here, make the plane what it is. If all the souls here were not so filled with malice, such a place would not exist."

"But it seems strange that they do not change their ways after leaving earth. It seems they would now see things in a new light and wish to see the beauties that could so easily be theirs," Helen said.

"They do not change their ways, anymore than we do," said Helen's mother. "We find ourselves just as we were when we lived on earth, so, they are the same. These people are just as slow to change their ways now, as they were when they lived in the earth body. Do not forget that they are the same person, unchanged by death. As they were in the earth life, so are they in their life after death. In time they may see the futility of continuing on with this sort of living. Some of them remain in this surrounding for a long period of time; while others very readily see the hopelessness of continuing on in their weak, sordid, way of living.

"On your plane, that fact was a pleasure to find; but here it is no cause for rejoicing. I guess that is why, as I saw these people, that I hoped that they, might be changed by death. Of course, it is only logical that all, both good, and bad, should remain unchanged by death," said Helen, a bit sorry that these people had been so undeserving.

"I know how you feel," said Helen's father. "That is why we try so hard to help them better themselves. It is unfortunate that they have filled their souls with this blackness; but it is even more unfortunate that they do nothing about it now. Now they see so plainly their undoing. And with all hindrances, that they might have been handicapped with on earth, taken away, there is no excuse or reason for them to continue having their souls filled with such hatred and malice."

"These people," said Helen's mother, "are masters of their own souls, and therefore, are responsible for their evil. it is within each of them to remain as they are, or find their rightful place."

"Yes I know," said Helen. "But you would think that they would be anxious to live under better conditions, instead of being satisfied to remain here."

"On earth haven't you often thought the same thing about people who chose a life of crime? Haven't you ever wondered why they would rather be a fugitive from justice, than living a normal happy life? It is the same with these people. They are no different. Some of them, like some on earth, do change their ways when the opportunity is given to them; but others cling to their old standard," Helen's father explained.

"People seem sometimes, to be so much alike, and still, we all react differently to the same things, said Helen. We live in the same world, contact the same things, but still individually, the effect of these outside influences have vastly different effects on each person. We each seem to respond to our surrounding with an entirely different outlook on life."

They had been walking along commenting on the pecularities of the human reactions, when they were approached by a man, who seemed franticly upset.

"Say mister. Could you help me?"

Helen's father stepped in front of the man who had approached him. "What seems to be the trouble? You seem quite upset."

The man wiped his hand across his brow, then nervously wrung his hands. He hardly knew how to go about this thing that weighed so heavily upon him. But he felt desperately in need for help of some kind.

"I'm going to lose my mind if this continues," he said. "Over and over again, like a terrible nightmare, I see all the terrible things I have done. I can't get away from it. No matter what I do, or where I go, my mind is filled with these awful things. I can't stand it! I tell you I can't stand it! For God's sake tell me how I can escape!"

"The first thing to do is to calm down and think this over quietly, said Helen's father. "You are only making matters worse by taking on so. Come, here, and sit down and tell me just what it is all about. Have you just recently come here?"

"I guess it has only been a matter of days. I don't know.

It seems endless since this troubling torment started. It's been like a moving picture of my life, constantly flashing before my eyes. At first I tried not to pay attention to it. God knows, I've been no saint! I never pretended to be one. But never until now, did I realize my cruelty. I was like a man on the loose. Oh I knew what I was doing! I gloried in my lack of feeling. I laughed at my crimes. Each new crime carried me on to another with a new zest. I had no time, nor inclination, then, to stop and think about what I was doing. I was too busy planning crimes to waste time with things already done."

"Was crime your profession?" asked Helen's father.

"Crime was my life. It was my every thought. I put my all, into it. Every waking hour, I spent either planning or doing. It was a business with me. I thought I was a great guy! No one could touch me ... Oh no! I had full protection. I never knew what fear was. I wasn't afraid of anything. Even now I'm not afraid. It's just that I can't stand seeing things as they really are. It is torture for me to think of what I have done. If I could only shut it out, just for a little while; but I can't get away from it. Isn't there some way I can black out this past, and find peace?" he asked.

"Yes, there is, said Helen's father. "But it is going to mean a lot of conscientious effort on your part."

"Anything would be better than what I am going through now. I can't stand much more of this. It is driving me mad! I'd do anything to be able to undo what I have done. But, they tell me that, that is impossible. If I can't undo it, how can I right it? If I could only go back and have another chance," he said.

"You can't go back," said Helen's father, "but you can

have another chance. What is your name?"

"Just call me Joe, that was what my mother always called me, and I want to forget the guy I thought I was. I didn't go by that name in my career of crime. Maybe that is the only kind thing I ever did for my mother. Heaven only knows, I didn't bring her any happiness. I can see that now. She is up there on one of the other planes and is getting her rightful reward."

"Has she been to see you?" asked Helen's mother.

"Yeah .... ", Joe said, smiling and shaking his head, as though he couldn't understand his mother's forgiveness. She was the one to greet me and bring me here. She wanted to help me then, but I wasn't ready to be helped. I guess that in itself was another hurt for her. I didn't realize it at the time. She has come to see me nearly every day since I have been here. I don't see how a guy like me, can be the son of the likes of her. That is another thing that torments me. I was always so thoughtless of her. I even let her die alone, just as I let her live alone in poverty and want, while I basked in luxuries. Now, she wants to do for me.

"Perhaps now you can reward her by your efforts to right your wrongs. That will bring her more joy than you can guess," said Helen's mother. "You are pretty well worn out from your ordeal. Supposing that we all go and refresh ourselves at the Cathedral."

"I've never been in a church since I was a small boy," Joe said. "Do you think I am fit to go in?"

"That is what the Churches are put here for," said Helen's father. "If God did not think there was need for them on this plane, they would not be here. It is there you will begin to see your way clear to accomplish what you desire to do. It is too bad that you have not found comfort and strength there before this."

"I haven't been able to do anything with all this turmoil inside of me. I have felt that I was in a whirlpool and could not swim against the current. I thought that I could battle it out in time, but it got the best of me just as you came along. I seem to feel better, though, just having talked to you. I have unburdened my load and some of the throbbing in my brain has stopped," Joe said.

"Well let's go inside and see if that doesn't relieve you some more." Helen's father patted Joe on the shoulder and smiled at him.

They remained in the Cathedral for some little time. Joe sat silent and felt that he never wanted to leave. For while he was there he found peace for the first time since coming into this world. Tears of thankfulness trickled down his cheeks. His shame and humiliation filled him with humbleness.

The others remained as long as Joe wished to stay. They were only too glad to help this soul find the solace and understanding that he was badly in need of.

Joe had built up a hard shell about his soul while living on earth. He had not allowed his soul to take much part in his earth life. He had lived by his physical brain, shutting out any feelings from within, until he had caused his soul to become so deeply buried and shut out from his activities that it had ceased to have any influence.

Now that Joe no longer had his physical body, his soul once more had full power. He was no longer able to push it into the background, for he was new all soul. It was for this reason that he felt so strongly the pangs of remorse.

Some souls grow completely blackened and weak, when housed in a body where the physical part of a man commits crimes against himself or the world. But if it is entirely the working of the physical brain that desires to do these things, and the soul itself is desirous to be better, then that soul still retains the power of feeling right from wrong. It is only submerged into a state of reticence.

This was the type of person that Joe had been. His physical brain had ruled his actions; while his soul struggled in vain for recognition.

At first Joe's crimes bothered him somewhat; but he had striven to overcome this weakness. It was only through battle, that he had come to the point of lack of feeling. It was then that his soul had been submerged into dormancy. Now, this soul was free from the physical, and eager to right all wrong, that it might once again, have the power to grow strong and flourish as it should. This was why Joe, now as a soul, felt the panic of his wrongdoings and was so duly remorseful.

Some souls do not battle against circumstances that come to them while in the earth body, and therefore the soul becomes sinful in itself. That is why some souls are unrepentant and decline any betterment.

Joe was suffering from his wrongdoing, and his soul was miserable in its present state. He wanted progression and the right to earn it.

As he sat in the Cathedral the way seemed clear to him. He would work as he had never done before, in order to right his every wrong. He knew that they were many, and the task that lay ahead of him was one of long toil. He had found himself now, in the quiet meditation in the Cathedral. No longer was he torn between the question of right and wrong. He knew now the way he must go and the things he must do. He raised his eyes and looked squarely into the eyes of Helen's father.

"I'm ready now," he said.

They rose and walked from the Cathedral. And as they did so a bright ray of light fell upon their pathway.

Joe wiped a tear of happiness from his eye, and said, "I know that I will be helped by that same power as I go my way. I have found comfort and understanding in this hour. I will be strong and unwavering as I right my wrongs."

"I am glad to see that you are ready to begin your progression. As long as you try, you will be helped along your way. The torment of your soul will decrease as you strive to live right in this world," said Helen's mother.

"Thank you," said Joe, "for your help", as he bade them goodbye.

"Well, there goes another soul on the right path," said Helen. "How differently they all react."

"Yes," said Helen's mother, "no two are exactly the same. We find all kinds here. Some ready for help; others contented as they are. It is entirely up to them whether they remain here, or go on to a better, fuller life." No one can decide that for them. Some of them will never try to wipe the blackness from their soul. But they will be forever doomed to this plane of darkness, unless they make amends.

"What kind of things will Joe have to do in order to earn the right to go on to a better way of living," Helen asked.

"That is not for us to say," said Helen's father. "The Divinity is the one to settle that. We do not judge, nor say what these souls must do. We help to show them the way and teach them the rules of this land. But the punishment and adjustment is in the hands of God."

"I was only wondering what they could do and how they would go about making up for the wrongs they have committed. Joe, for instance, he seems so young. I don't believe he can be over thirty-five at the most. He certainly did not have a very long earth life. It is too bad that he chose a life of crime. He seems to have a great deal of intelligence for a character of that kind. I always associated a man of that kind with being rough and harsh spoken. If one didn't know, he could pass for a gentleman. He speaks well, and when he isn't upset, his mannerisms are pleasing," said Helen.

"There are all types," said Helen's father. "Joe would be what is known as a 'smoothie'." "That type of person is the most dangerous of all, because people so little suspect the kind of person he really is. They trust him and therefore, fall prey to his cunningness."

"Joe can't undo the things that he did while on earth, therefore it is hard for me to understand just how he will go about righting those wrongs," said Helen.

"That will be a long steady task," Helen's mother said. I

can theorize, to give you some idea of how he will go about it; but I cannot say specifically, for as I have said, that is between Joe and God. I do know, however, that the first thing that he will have to do is to learn the laws that rule here. He will learn these things from the teachers from the higher planes, whose work it is to help these souls.

He will attend lectures conducted by these teachers. There he will be taught how to gain wisdom and the powers of God. They will teach him how to use his soul for good, and cast out all evil. After he has learned how to conduct his soul along these lines, then he will attend classes where he will be taught ways of making himself useful in this world or on earth. Not until this educational period is completed, will he be ready and fit to start his work."

"The next step then, is when he is assigned to his special work. He owes a debt to humanity on earth, where he abused his rights. Therefore, he may return to that sphere, as a soul, to now be of help to humanity. He must give some good, to the people on earth life, in order to pay for the wrong he did them while he lived there. For instance, for a life that he took with his own hands, he may be called upon to endure some of the hardships that he brought on by this death. In case he took the life of a family, he would find it in his fate to go back and help that family in their adjustments. He would suffer their sorrows with them. He would see little children want for food, and be deprived of their father's love. It would be up to him to guard them from harm, and to find some way to help lighten the burden. In this way, he would in some small measure, be helping humanity."

"Step by step throughout the years, he will slowly right his wrongs by serving humanity. His tasks will be many and varied, his progress slow, until he has paid full penance."

"He will be called upon to do certain things on this plane. Such as working to wipe out the evil in these people. There will be many things for him to study as he goes along. From time to time he will spend a certain portion of time with the teachers from the other planes. In this way he will learn new ways of helping."

"His privileges will be increased from time to time, as he helps humanity. When he is deserving, he will then be allowed to progress to the next plane. By that time he will have righted his great wrongs and learned the happiness of doing for others. He will be eager to reach higher goals, and will then seek ways to learn more so that he might continue his progression.

"It is a long process, but in the end it is well worth the effort. God's methods are fair and just. And everyone has an equal chance."

"It is so much easier to do wrong, than to right it," said Helen.

"Yes," said Helen's father, "but it is still easier if you try to live a good life."

Helen laughed at her father's remark. She had been carried away by the unfoldment of Joe's life ahead, and had been filled with a feeling of despondency. Now she laughed and joked with her parents as they went on their way.

They passed a group of people gathered together, and they were singing in loud voices. When they finished the song, they burst into laughter. They seemed to be enjoying themselves, and were having some sort of party. Now they sang,"For he's a Jolly Good Fellow." Helen said, "They seem to be enjoying themselves."

"Oh yes," said Helen's mother, "they have their moments of happiness. Some of them do not seem to mind being here at all. They are giving a welcoming party to a new arrival and are glad to have him join them."

Helen smiled at their apparent happiness. She couldn't see how they could be so happy to have anyone come to this plane. But she supposed that it was only natural to like to have your friends with you, wherever you were.

Helen noticed her dress for the first time since coming to this plane. She couldn't understand the change in color. It had been a beautiful shade of blue; but now it was a yellowish brown color. She glanced at her mother's apparel; it too had changed to this drab color.

"Mother, what happened to our clothing?"

Her mother smiled. "Nothing really. They have just taken on the drabness of the surroundings."

"But we are not of this plane. Why should we have to wear drab looking clothing?" asked Helen.

"The colors that we have on our plane can not exist here. "The atmosphere here is different, due to the conditions, which produce a chemical that dissolves our colors. You have undoubtedly heard the old saying, that when a person becomes very angry, he throws off a poison into his system. Well it is very much like that here. These people throw out an atmosphere of hatred, evil, and sullenness. Of course, you noticed that in the beginning by the heaviness of the air. It is dense and smokey, and hangs like a cloud of fog. The same influences that cause that, cause the change in coloring of our clothing."

"But our souls are not touched nor darkened by our being here, "Helen said.

"No, we are shielded and protected from that, " said Helen's father. "We still retain our radiance. That is how you can so readily tell the souls from the higher planes. They are like a light in the dark. It's like seeing one happy smiling face in a group of grief stricken people. That one smiling face will send a ray of brightness through the whole room."

"I am beginning to understand some of the ways of this world, said Helen. "Everything seems to have a purpose for its existence."

"Every thing, and everyone," said Helen's mother. "We all serve some purpose, in one way or another." "Is that a church ahead?" asked Helen.

"Yes would you like to see one of the churches? It is different you know, than the Cathedral or the house of solace. There you go specifically for strength and Divine wisdom. The churches are more like those on Earth. Services of worship are held here very much the same as they are on Earth."

"Do they have a minister?" asked Helen.

"They have visiting ministers, or rather teachers, who come from time to time from the higher realms to lead the people in worship. There is no set one, who has a church for a given length of time. Nor is he in any sense, a judge with higher authority. He is only a scholar of the teachings of God. He comes to enlighten the people with the knowledge that he has gained."

"It seems to be empty. Oh no, there is a man down in front arranging some flowers. Who is he?" Helen asked.

"He is one of the ministers. Perhaps there is to be a service here today, early morning service," said Helen's father.

"Is it morning already?" "I guess time does go fast here," Helen laughed.

"Oh, there is a woman going down the outside isle," said Helen's mother. "She is early." "Would you like to stay for the service or shall we wait and attend one on our own plane?"

"Let's wait until we return to your own church," said Helen. I think that I would enjoy that more.

They were just about to leave the church, when Helen turned at the sound of a woman's whining voice. She was lamenting her fate to the minister and carrying on in tones of bewailment.

"She feels that she has been unfairly judged," said Helen's mother. "Perhaps you would like to remain and learn of this type of person before we go on to the second plane."

Helen hesitated about remaining. It seemed to her that

she had seen about enough of the people on this plane, but hearing this woman's grievances interested her. She had never dreamed that such things would be allowed. She slid into the back pew, along side her parents and listened.

The minister was welcoming her and trying to understand her troubles. At first he thought that she was early for the service, and wanted to make her welcome. But as the woman went on talking in her whining voice, he soon learned otherwise.

"I came to see you before your service begins," she said. "I want you to do a favor for me. I have been misjudged and wronged by being sent here to this plane, and I want you to speak to someone about it.

The minister smiled at her and asked her to sit down beside him. "I am afraid that you misunderstand," he said. "I am only here to minister unto the people; I have no right to interfere in God's Judgment. I will be glad to do anything to help but, as for acting as a spokesman, I am afraid that would be out of the question.

"Well but you are a minister, and you should be able to intervene for me to God. A minister always rights things for a person with God. And that is what I want you to do."

"No one is capable of righting himself with God, but you," said the minister.

"But I have been wronged. I am a good Christian woman. I spent my whole life in devotion to saving other souls. I do not belong here with these wicked people. I want to be taken to my Father in Heaven and set this right. There has been a grave mistake. I am not happy here in this desolate gloomy place. I should rightfully be with the angels," she related.

"Only God is the judge of that. He, alone, knows the justice of a thing," said the minister gently. "We do not question His wisdom, nor do we retract his judgment. We can only hope to be of help in clearing up a situation of this kind. Supposing that you tell me something of the circumstances, and perhaps I will be able to explain the reason for your being here."

"Well I know it is a mistake. You will see that, when I tell you of my life. I was always good and working for God. I was his servant and served him well."

"Tell me of some of the things that you did in this service. Just what did you do?" asked the minister.

"Well I did so many things I hardly know where to begin," she said, in a martyr like way. "But I always went to church and prayed for the poor sinners. Then there was the time that I took upon myself the duty to see that Mrs. Brown's child would have the religious training that it had been denied."

"Just how did you go about this?" the minister asked her, beginning to see why she had come to live on the dark plane.

"The first thing that I did, was to report her to the town authorities, as being an unfit mother. You see, she worked and couldn't give her children the proper care. They were never sent to Sunday School nor taught the finer things of life. A person like that has no right to have children," she went on.

"What was the outcome?" asked the minister.

"The authorities claimed there was no cause for action.

They said that she gave them love and proper care. And that she did not neglect them in any way, so that they could not take her children from her. They said that everyone had the right to attend church, or not, as they saw fit. But as she was a neighbor of mine, I saw to it myself, that she learned the errors of her ways," she said.

"And just how did you accomplish this?" he asked.

"Well, I just went over there and told her a thing or two! And I'm proud to tell you that she sent her children to Sunday School after that," she said, airily.

"Then" she continued, "there was the time I headed the committee to have our minister removed. He was unfit to fulfill such a sacred office. Why, do you know that he sanctioned smoking and card playing! Well we got rid of him!

He wasn't ousted entirely, but he was moved to another state. We wanted no part of him in our church! I saw my duty and I did it. Now do you see why I know that there has been a miscarriage of justice?"

The minister sat silent for a full moment. Then he said, "I greatly regret what I am going to have to tell you. In your effort to do good, you have created the biggest sin of all. It is true that you were a member of a church, but that in itself is not enough. We must live up to what we profess to be. That is where you fell down. The most important commandment in the bible, you broke. 'Judge not, lest you be judged also'."

"Instead of doing good, you did others a great injustice. No man who walks the face of the earth has the right to tell others what is right and what is wrong, according to his own belief. None of us are infallible, and therefore have no right to judge. "

"Then you think I am getting my just dues! Well I'll tell you, that no one lived a better life on earth than I did! I only saw my duty and did it. Why I was God's servant," she whined, hoping still to have him help her make arrangements to be rejudged.

"Perhaps if you had gone about it differently, you would not be here. Instead of living your life to the best of your ability, you were more concerned about the lives of other people. That was where you committed your greatest sin. Now God is judging you accordingly. You judged others more for the sake of appearing righteous before them, than for the good you could bring them. We are only responsible for our own actions. Wherefore you alone, will be judged for taking it into your own hands to judge others.

"Perhaps now that you understand the reason for your being here, you will try to rectify it," the minister pointed out.

The woman was angry now and flared up at him. She saw that she had been unsuccessful in her attempt to whimper sympathy from him. She had known in her heart all along, why she had found herself in this state, but had hoped in some way to bring about a change without having to work for it.

"Rectification!" she shouted. "That's all you hear around this plane. There is no justice! I'll stay here until I rot, before I'll believe that you or anybody else lived a more upright life than I did. And you can tell those high and mighty people that come from other planes, just that," she said as she flaunted out of the church.

Helen looked at her parents in bedwilderment. How did this woman dare to defy God in such a manner. How could she question His judgment.

"Don't look so startled," said her father, as they left the church. That just proves there are all kinds of people here. And that leaving their physical body does not change their personality one iota."

"Well, I never would have believed it if I hadn't seen it," Helen said. "Wasn't she high and mighty though, when she found that he wasn't going to arrange for her betterment?"

"That's the attitude that some of them take. Especially when they have always been used to having the upper hand and telling others what to do and what not to do," said Helen's mother.

"Would you like to look in on Paul for a minute?" "He should be up and ready to go to the hospital by now."

"Yes, and I'd like to see how I'm getting along," Helen giggled. "I can't lose interest in my body, as soon I will return to it."

Chapter VII

"This means of travel is delightful," said Helen. There is only one thing that it makes me think of."

"And what is that?" asked her mother, seeing that something had amused Helen.

"Well we decide we want to go to Earth to see Paul." "And what do we do," she said impishly. "We just say alright we will now, and the first thing you know, there we are!"

"But what does it make you think of?" her father asked, eager for his daughter's impression.

"It's like being on the top floor of a big building, and suddenly deciding that you want to go to the main floor. You walk to the elevator going down, and before you know it, you are on the first floor. Only, here, you don't feel as though the bottom of the earth has suddenly fallen from under you, like you do in an elevator. Nor have your heart feel like it is up in your throat."

Helen laughed, and her eyes were bright with merriment.

"The comparison seems to amuse you, " said her mother. "But I must admit, that it explains it pretty well. Only as you said, there is no sensation with our means of travel. I am afraid that we wouldn't hold up very well, if we had the sensation of riding an elevator all day, with the amount of traveling we do. Personally, I'd soon feel seasick. I never was very partial to riding elevators, especially the fast ones."

Helen and her parents were in good spirits after their jovial banter. Fact was, they were a little on the silly side by the time they entered the hospital room.

Paul was there, having stopped in on his way to the office. He looked much better after his night's rest.

Helen went over to him and put her arms around him and gave him a big hug, and kissed him. She had gotten used to being ignored by earth people and it did not bother her so much now. It rather amused her this morning as she was feeling in such good spirits. She laughed as she gave his hair a tug.

"This isn't so hard to take once you get used to the idea," she said, her eyes twinkling.

"You certainly are in good spirits this morning," said her father. "Well, we have had quite a lot of fun at that. One might just as well see the funny side of things as to brood over them."

Paul had taken his coat off and had settled down to sit by the side of Helen's physical body. He looked at her quietly lying there, and spoke to the nurse.

"Has the doctor come in this morning?" he asked.

"He was in about an hour ago, but said that he would stop back later to see you. Your wife had an uneventful night and seems to be some better this morning," the nurse told him.

"But she hasn't rallied?" asked Paul.

"No, but her condition seems to be much better. The doctor has the reports of the tests he made and was quite encouraged. He should be along soon now," the nurse said.

"She does look a little better this morning," said Paul. "She doesn't seem quite as drawn looking, she has a little more color."

"That is a good indication," said the nurse. "It looks now as though we could look for a recovery from this coma most any time. Were you planning to stay here at the hospital today?"

"Why yes. I couldn't accomplish anything if I did go to the office. I called them and told them I wouldn't be in today," said Paul .

"But he will," said Helen's father, smiling wisely at his daughter.

"And just how do you know so much?" asked Helen, good naturedly.
"Ah! That is where I have one on you," replied Helen's father, teasingly. "I suppose that you think in your short visit with us that you have learned all there is to know about our ways! You are still in kindergarten," he laughed.

"Stop your teasing," said Helen, "and tell me, how do, you know?"

"Your father seems to be enjoying mystifying you," said Helen's mother. "So I will tell you."

"It is possible for us to see what the immediate future holds. When we come in close contact with those who live on Earth, their problems and there outcome is visualized by us. That is how we are able to help, and advise. If it were not for this being possible, we would have no more foresight in the matter than Paul has. It is though a picture of the past, present and future had been taken, and shown to us. Each person has a background on which these pictures are shown. We call it a person's cycle. In this cycle is shown events that will take place. In this way we are prepared for whatever comes to this person, and act accordingly."

"Now it shows plainly, that Paul will not remain at the Hospital as he expects to. After he talks to the Doctor, he will feel so much better, that he will see the uselessness of his remaining. He will go to his office and there remain the rest of the day. You wait and see."

The Doctor came into the room and Helen and her parents listened to the conversation between Paul and the Doctor.

"Good morning, Paul," the Doctor said. "I have a bit of good news for you this morning. Helen is doing nicely and her troubles will soon be over. We have examined her thoroughly, and are very encouraged."

"What did you find?" asked Paul.

"Well the first X-rays that we took last night, showed a clot very close to the base of her brain. That was very disturbing to me as there was a possibility that it might go directly to the brain. In that case, it would become more complicated and serious. Now the clot is only causing a pressure on a nerve leading to the brain which is causing this coma. However, it seemed advisable this morning to check to see which way the clot was moving, if at all. Therefore we took another picture and found that the clot had decreased in size and had moved a little to the left. That accounts for her better color today. We have hopes, and every reason to believe, that this clot will dissolve. And that, my man, is good news."

"Then she will come out of this coma?" Paul asked.

"Then she will be as good as new again," the Doctor assured him. "I have hopes that it may clear up all the trouble she has been having. It is just possible, that this same clot has existed in other regions, during her trouble with her heart. If so, that would account for the strain that was put on her heart. Now if it is dissolved, her heart will once again function normally, and she will be perfectly well."

"I hope so," said Paul grinning. "It certainly would be worth all of this to have her well again. She does, look better."

"Well I must be getting along," said the Doctor. If you are going now, I will walk along with you. I suppose you are pretty busy at the office these days?"

"Yes we are way behind," said Paul. "But I had intended to stay here with Helen and not go to the office today."

"Well do just as you like, but I see no call for your

staying here. It would be better for you to go on with your work. It is rather tedious being cooped up in a Hospital all day. And you certainly won't be helping her any. All we can do now is wait for the clot to dissolve. She is having medicine now that will help accomplish this. Come along and go with me."

Helen went over to Paul and gave him a push, playfully. "Get along and do as the Doctor says," she said.

Helen's parents laughed at her. She seemed so full of 'the old harry' today. She certainly was enjoying herself, and they were happy that she had been able to come and be with them.

They watched her now with great delight. Helen was rather tall and dark, and her dark eyes were sparkling with mischievousness as she went on plaguing Paul. Her slender body was rythmical in its every movement. She had always been graceful, even in her early childhood. Helen's parents had always marveled at the nature of their child. One moment she would be sedate and queenly; while in the flash of an eye, she would suddenly act like a clown. It was these characteristics that made her so lovable. Paul on the other-hand, was broad shouldered, solid, and fair. He was most always clowning; except on occasions such as this, and then he was most serious. It was rarely that Paul looked on the somber side of life. He and Helen were well suited, and made a fine looking couple.

Paul picked up his coat and said, "0. K. Maybe you are right. I guess I may just as well go on down to the office and get my work underway, as to sit here, if I can't be of any help." "Nurse, you have my telephone number in case you want to get in touch with me. Call me if she regains consciousness," Paul said, as he and the Doctor went out the door.

Helen said, "Well let's go too. It looks as though I might have to come back soon now, so I better get on with my exploring."

"By the way! If you can see what is to happen, then why couldn't you see that the blood clot would dissolve?" asked Helen.

"Well we told you that there was every chance that you would return to earth, and if you did you would find that you were much better than you had been. We also told you that you were not fully released from your body, and proved that to you.

"The Doctors from our land were in charge of the physical condition, and therefore we left that part up to them. We could have delved into that part of it, had we wanted to. But we were more concerned with showing you our world. That was our part of taking care of you. We each are interested in a different phase of your life and therefore are only interested in foreseeing the part that affects our work," said Helen's father.

"Yes I can understand that," said Helen, becoming more serious now. But did you say, that you did not know for sure whether or not I would return to earth life."

"That is true," said Helen's mother. "We did not know, and were not allowed to know. Some things are withheld from our vision; things that are not best for us to know at the time. If it is in any way connected to the outcome, and we could do something to help, then we would be shown. But in this case it would neither have been of any consequence nor best."

"But I can't see why it would have made any difference if we had known what the outcome was to be," said Helen. "You said that no one knew for certain, but the High Power. Why then, didn't He let it be shown in my cycle?"

"Until now, it was not for us to know," said Helen's mother. "Some things are held from our eyes for a purpose, and this was one of them. Some things show up clearly in your cycle for a long ways ahead. Other things only become visual as the time is right. There is a purpose for it all."

"Think of it this way," said Helen's father. "If you had been told in the beginning, that you were not to go back to live in your physical body, the shadow of this fact would have caused you great sympathy for Paul. You would not, as you have, enjoyed your visit here with such enthusiasm. Now then, had it turned out that your physical body was no longer capable of housing your soul, and it ceased to function, and you were now fully released from that body, it would have served no purpose to have foreseen it. It would only have foreshadowed the grief that would have come to Paul, and cast a sympathetic feeling over you, that was unnecessary.

"Now it is shown clearly that you are to go back into your physical body and go on with your earth life. The time is right now for us to know this, and so we are shown."

"Then it was really to my benefit not to know. I can understand now, but before there seemed no purpose in not telling us."

"There may also be underlying reasons for withholding

this until now, that we will never know. It may have been the wisdom of God, to balance the practicality of the restoration of your body. We do not question His ways, nor his decisions," said Helen's mother.

As they walked down the street, Helen saw a friend of hers. She went over and spoke to her before she thought. When Margaret made no reply, Helen remembered that she was invisible to Margaret's eyes, and that she did not hear her.

Helen wanted to do something to attract her attention so she pushed against Margaret's arm, causing her to drop her purse. This was quite an accomplishment, but Helen did not know just how she had done it. She would tell Margaret about it when she came back to live in her physical body.

"I believe Margaret is on her way to the Hospital to see me," Helen told her parents. "I got that thought from her. That must be because she is thinking of me."

"Margaret is such a good friend,' said Helen's mother.

"Wait until I tell her about meeting her on the street. I'll bet that she won't believe me. You know, I'll bet that they will all think that my illness has left me a bit touched when I tell them of my experience," Helen said, quite amused.

"It may not be so amusing when you try to convince them of the truth of it," said Helen's father. People are very skeptical about life after death and that you remain the same. It will not be easy to convince them that you really did see this world with your own eyes," said Helen's father.

"I'll convince them or die trying," said Helen. How can

they doubt it when I tell them of all these things."

"It is more the nature of people to doubt a thing, that they cannot see for themselves, than it is to believe it," said Helen's mother. "You will find how true that is when you return to earth," she laughed.

"Yes, I hadn't thought just how far fetched it would seem to them. It is all so very real to me, but I suppose it will not seem so simple to them. Some things are still a little confusing to me," Helen said. "By the way, how did I manage to knock Margaret's purse from under her arm? I have tried to move physical objects before, but have had very little success."

"Are you referring to the comb episode?" Her father laughed, as he remembered his daughter's bewilderment with that experience.

"It wasn't funny at the time," said Helen. "How did I know that this hand of mine was not able to pick up physical objects. It looked the same and felt the same. I could use it on my own person. It was only that darn comb that I couldn't seem to lift."

"That was because you did not know how. It is possible to move an object of earth; but first you must learn how," said Helen's mother. It is not so very difficult after you master the technique. It will be better to show you how this is done later, when we may attend a class on this subject. It will then be much clearer to you."

"But," said Helen, "I did manage to make Margaret drop her purse. That was what I wanted to do and so gave her arm a push. I wanted to have some fact to bring to her attention when I go back and tell her of my experience. I thought if I could tell her of the incident of her dropping her purse, then she would have to believe that I was there and saw it." Helen wanted her friend to really understand her experiences.

"That will, be a help in convincing her," said Helen's mother. But the push on the arm that you gave her, was not so much responsible for her dropping her purse, as was your desire to make her drop it. You more or less planted the thought of dropping it in her mind. And as she went to move her arm to adjust it more securely, it fell. However, you were the cause of it falling, and so fulfilled your desire and aim."

"There are many different ways of making your presence felt," said her father. "It is only a matter of learning how to accomplish these things, and in time we all do. Some means of manifestation is more complicated than others. And many of us do not bother to learn these more difficult accomplishments. It is our privilege to take them or leave them, just as are many other things in this life.

"We are not all interested in the same things, anymore than we were while living on Earth. That is why you will find people doing what most interests them. Some people over here do not have much inquisitiveness and therefore do not investigate into things. It is just like the Earth people. Some of them never stop learning and progressing; while others are perfectly contented with their meager amount of knowledge. We find the same thing is true over here. Many of them are so pleased with conditions that they find here, that they are satisfied to accept them without delving into it deeper. They have their home, family, and friends and pleasant living conditions. Beyond that, there is no more to be desired on their part. They find complete satisfaction in living in their own scope."

"Well I have a natural curiosity," said Helen. "I guess I was born with the desire to investigate things."

"Yes I guess you were," said her mother. "From the time you could get around you wanted to see what made things work. You were forever asking questions. And it didn't make any difference what came up, you wanted to know what it was all about. And I might say, that you haven't changed with the years."

"Oh my," said Helen as she looked about her, "How true those words are going to be. This must be the second plane that we are on now, and I will prove how right you are when you say that I am still a question box."

"You ask all the questions that you want to. We enjoy having you with us and we haven't much longer to be able to answer your questions so directly," Helen's mother said, patting her daughter caressingly.

Chapter VIII

"This is a nice place," said Helen as she looked all around. "I could be quite happy here myself. Of course it isn't quite as nice as the plane you live on. But it is certainly a great improvement over the low plane. There is nice sunlight and beauty here. The coloring is a little less outstanding than on your plane, but as a whole, I think this is pretty nice."

"Yes, the second plane is a pleasant place," said Helen's mother.

"There aren't so many children on these planes as I saw on your plane. I don't believe that I have seen any children."

"Children do not start their life, as a soul, on either of these planes. They are taken directly to the higher planes. A child has lived such a short time on earth that he is not touched by shortcomings. A small child on earth remains pretty much a soul of God. Until he grows older and lives in closer contact with ugliness and temptation, he is untouched by its marks. Therefore he is still more spiritual than physical up to a certain point. That is why you see no small children in the lower planes. Occasionally you will find a teenage child on this plane, but it is under rare circumstances. Such as a child who started early on a career of crime," Helen's father explained.

"How large are these planes?" Helen asked.

"Oh my! That is a question! I might say in answer to that, how big is the Earth?" said Helen's father.

"You seem to have baffled your father with that question," Helen's mother laughed. "Perhaps I can answer it by putting it like this; our world here is like a ceiling over your earth world. It is the same size as far as circumference. Its depth, I have no conception of, for I have not yet reached its ceiling. Each plane covers the circumference of the Earth. Its depth is vast, and each plane has as vast an atmosphere, as has Earth surrounding, it. That will give you some idea of the extensive territory that each plane covers."

"Then this plane, and all planes stretch the distance of all earth lands." said Helen.

"That is right," said Helen's mother. "You might think of it as each continent and locality having its own Heaven; or ceiling."

"Then you mean that people in Europe, Asia, and the Americas have a separate Heaven?" Helen asked.

"You might put it that way. But in a true sense it is all one Heaven. As I have said, each plane extends as a ceiling over the Earth world. There is no discrimination in their reward. All nationalities fare the same, according to their deserving as individuals. It is only natural that they would want to go to Heaven closest to where they had lived their earth life. They have many people still on earth in whom they are still interested. It is not that they could not contact them, were they living in our locality; but rather that they are happier in a Heaven made up of their own people who have the same customs and likes that they have. Perhaps you would like to visit the second plane of one of these foreign countries. In that way you would understand clearer just what I mean'" Helen's mother said. .'Oh I would like that, if it is possible," said Helen's father. "We can visit, or if we choose, take up permanent residence in any of these Heavens. But of course we would only be permitted to have the privilege of living on the plane that we are now living on. That is, until we had progressed on."

"Have you any preference?" Helen's mother asked.

"Helen thought for a moment. Then said, "China! Or ..... perhaps, England. I would be better able to understand the language there." Helen laughed.

"We have a Universal language here, so that won't make any difference," Helen's mother told her. "It is just a matter of choice on your part."

"You mean, that you have a language here that everyone can understand?" asked Helen, quite surprised at this revelation.

"Yes, thought," said Helen's mother, amused that her daughter had forgotten this means of communication. "The thought behind any spoken words is translated into a language that all who live here understand. For instance, if I should ask for a flower, no matter in what language I used, I still would have the thought of obtaining that flower. Do you see?"

"Yes," said Helen, smiling at the logicalness of it. It stands to reason, that whether we speak French or English that we convey the same thought. I never thought of that before. It's like speaking in one tongue, and having it translated for you so so that you understand the thought that the spoken words convey."

"That's it exactly!" said Helen's father. "Now you have the idea."

"Well then let's make it China!" Helen said, excitedly.

"China, it is then," her father said.

"Will it take long to get there?" asked Helen.

"Does it take long to get to Earth, or these other planes?" asked her father.

"Well no. No time at all. But China!" Helen said, thinking of how far away China was.

"Well we can project ourselves there just as quickly as we can any other place," said Helen's mother smiling. "The distance makes no difference whatsover. In cases of this kind, we travel by thought. We desire to be in China, and we are in, China. This sounds rather magical, I know. But in reality, it isn't at all. A person living in the earth body can very easily sit and think of a place, either that he has heard of, or visited. And as he thinks of this place, he can visualize it mentally. If he has been, say for instance, in someone's home, he can sit in his own home and visualize things as they were in that home. In the case that he has not been in a place, he mentally pictures what he thinks it would be like. And in a sense, he is, in his mind's eye, there. Now then when you think that this is possible on earth, it does not seem quite so strange that we here, as a soul, and unhampered by physical things, can actually transport ourselves to the desired place, by this same means of thought. Instead of being carried away in, thought; we are carried away, by, thought; and just as quickly as a physical person can think of a thing."

"Mother, you have such a way, of making things sound so simple. Well let's think ourselves to China then," said Helen jokingly.

"Oh my! What a change," said Helen.

"A change in the appearance of the surroundings; but it is fundamentally the same, as the second plane in the vicinity that we just left. These people enjoy the same privileges that the people back there do. It is only that these people have different tastes. Have you ever visited China town on earth and noticed their ways of living? Well here you see the real China. Their dress, their buildings and customs are strictly Chinese. They would feel strange and unhappy to be taken to a world where they would have to accustom themselves to a strange way of living," Helen's mother said.

"Then do all Chinese people, regardless of where they have been living on earth, come to Chinese Heaven to live with their own people, or whatever plane they rate?" Helen asked.

"Not necessarily," said Helen's mother. "For you see there are a great many Chinese people living in other Countries who have been weaned away from their homeland. There are even those who have been born and raised in other Countries, and they would feel strange in these surroundings. It is largely up to the individual and his desires. If he has family and friends here in this locality that he wishes to be with, then he would naturally be happier here. But if he feels no attachment for his native land, and their ways of living; then he would go to the plane, or ceiling, of his earth locality. There he would find many of his own race. Of course he could, whenever he wished, visit China and the Heavenly spheres of China.

"Do these various races intermingle in Heaven?" asked Helen.

"Oh yes! We often find ourselves interested in the same things and are thrown together by mutual interests. There is no discrimination. We are all souls of God and have equal rights. However, the people themselves choose to congregate with people of their own kind. That is as true on Earth as it is here, and only natural," said Helen's mother.

"We will show you when we return to our own plane," said Helen's father. "We will take you to visit the Indian tribes. They even have separate groups of Indians within their own territory. This is because they each have different customs and want to be with those who do things in their way. That should not be so difficult for you to understand.".

"No it seems very logical," said Helen. "It is just as Paul and I prefer certain groups of people. It is not that the other people in our vicinity are not just as good; but that we know, the friends that we have and therefore have common interests through frequent association." "It is very pretty here," said Helen's father. It seems a bit quaint to us, but that is what makes it an interesting place."

"Oh I love to visit places where the customs are different," said Helen. "Isn't the clothing pretty that they wear here? Such beautiful decorations of embroidery. It is strange that each country has its own style of dress. I guess that is our ways, and habits of living, that distinguish each country."

"It is what makes traveling interesting," said Helen's mother. "You will notice though, that outside of their different architecture and customs; that they have, and enjoy the same freedom of life and privileges that we found on the other part of this plane."

"Yes they seem to be living their normal life," said Helen, and seem to be just as happy and contented as the other people in the other localities of this plane. This is their Heaven, and as you said, they would not be happy in the strangeness of an unfamiliar surrounding. After being here, I can understand just how difficult it would be to accustom themselves to a new way of life. I know that this all seems strange to me, and I would feel lost to suddenly find myself living in this surroundings.

"You have not told me about the people who live on the second plane," said Helen. "Just why are they here?"

"There isn't a great deal to tell, except that they came to their rightful place, according to the way they lived," said Helen's father.

"But what sort of things did they do, that kept them from going to one of the higher planes?" Helen asked.

"It is more what they didn't do," said Helen's father, laughingly. "It isn't always because we do things that we shouldn't but that we don't do things that we should. Some of these people of course, are from the low plane and have progressed this far. The others, came here directly from earth. The people you find on this plane have not lived a wicked life; but rather a weak life. By that I mean, that they failed to do that which they were capable of doing. We do not have to do great things while we live our earth life, nor try to be Saints. None of us is perfect, nor near perfect, and were not intended to be. We are only human and therefore subject to failings. But we are supposed, while in our Earth life, or in this life, to contribute something for the good of humanity. However some of us are selfish and self-centered and live for ourselves alone. For such a life, there is not such a high reward, as for the one who thinks of his fellow-man and does many deeds of kindness. It is not that those who live on the second plane have done any great wrong; but that they have done very little good. Therefore until they have the willingness to be kind and generous to those whom they associate with, their own life will not be so generously considered. They get, only, as they give," Helen's father explained.

"That seems just enough," said Helen. "I'll bet that you and mother were glad that you were always so kind and generous."

''Ah! But that is where we failed too," said Helen's mother.

"Haven't you always been on the third plane since you left earth life?" Helen asked, with great surprise.

"Yes we were very fortunate to have deserved the beauties of the third plane. But the great majority of people enter the third plane when their life on earth is completed," said Helen's mother.

"That should bolster your faith in humanity," said Helen's father. "There are more good people than bad, we are happy to say. Not many are called upon to live on the low plane; only those who have wronged society, greatly. The second plane consists largely of those who have made progress, and also those who have lived an unusually selfish undermining Earth life."

"But there are so many people here and on the low plane just in the particular part where we visited," said Helen, not fully understanding.

"It stands to reason that when you gather them all together that they appear to be numerous. But in reality that is not true, when you consider the numerous people that there are in the world. Supposing for instance, that you took two people out of each city, and one out of each smaller community. When you had them all gathered together from every part of the globe, you would find that you had quite a multitude. However, it would be a very small percentage of the people. That is why I say that very few people from Earth are compelled to live on the low plane after death."

"I see what you mean," said Helen. "But you mentioned that you failed in many ways to live as good a life as you were capable of living. I do not believe that I understand that. You were the most thoughtful people that I ever came in contact with. You were always fair and just, and generous as the day was long."

"Even if that were true," said Helen's mother, "we could have spread a great deal more happiness as we went along. it is the things that you don't do, the little kindnesses that we overlook in our busy lives that count. Why, do you know one of the things that bothered my conscious the most after I came here to live?"

"No what was it?" Helen asked inquisitively.

"Well now you may laugh when I tell you, but it certainly caused me many unhappy moments," said Helen's mother.

She felt selfconscious now that she was about to tell Helen. It did seem like water under the bridge after such a long time. But it really had hit her like a bolt of lightning, when she realized after the many years, the hurt and sorrow that she must have caused her mother.

"Well come on tell me! Don't keep me in suspense," Helen said.

Her mother smiled, and then began. "Well I was quite a young lady then, it was during my courting days with your father. He had asked me to go to a dance that his fraternity was giving. I wanted to go the worst way, for I had never been to a dance, though I had learned to dance from the girls at school. When I asked my mother's permission, she refused to let me go. Of course, I had known that my mother opposed to those public dances that the young folks enjoyed so much, but I had thought that she might relent and let me go. She did not believe in dancing to begin with. She had been taught that it was sinful, and good christians did not take part, nor sanction it. My heart was broken and I became angry. I told her in loud terms that she was narrow and mean. That there was no sin in dancing except what she saw through her own evil eyes. And that she was herself possessed by the Devil to keep me from going and enjoying myself with the others. I then flung myself on the bed and had a good cry. She let me cry it out without reprimanding me in any way. When I had calmed down, she tried to comfort me and make me understand that she was only thinking of my welfare. She was so gentle with me that I felt ashamed of myself and told her how sorry I was for my outburst. I never again in all my years talked back to my mother. But the remembrance of that night has since caused my heart to ache with remorse."

Helen threw her head back and laughed and laughed in spite of her mother's seriousness in telling the story.

"I just can't picture your going into a rage. You of all people!" Helen said. I never even saw you become ruffled, no matter what the circumstances."

"Well but remember," said her mother, I was young then and had not learned to control myself. Besides, I was in love and resented being treated like a child. I think my dignity was hurt more than anything," Helen's mother chuckled.

"All children have fits of anger and take it out on their parents when they feel abused," said Helen. "I know that I have."

"Yes and the mother forgives them and knows that in their heart they do not mean what they say or do. When they are older, of course these things hurt; but their love for their child overshadows the hurt, and is put aside," said Helen's mother.

"But after all those years still your conscious bothered you? "

"Yes" said Helen's mother. "And I could not rid myself

of it until I had in some small measure made amends to my mother."

"How could you do this?" Helen asked. "Your mother came here to live before you did, so what means did you have of making it up to her?"

"There was only one way that I could, and that was to create as much happiness for her as I could. Like going on excursions through this beautiful land. And taking her to see things that she had never seen before. We traveled the planes here, and places of beauty on Earth that she had always been desirous of seeing. It was not that she could not have done these things without me, but more that she wanted me along. It seemed to add to her enjoyment," Helen's mother related.

"There is one thing that your mother is omitting," said Helen's father. "And that is, that she gave up her own interests in order to go with her mother at that particular time. I remember well, that she was devoting most of her time with babies and small children who had come into this world. She loved the work that she had taken upon herself to do, and was keenly interested in the study of their development. It was really a sacrifice on your mother's part to pick up and leave at that particular stage of her on soul growth."

"Then did you feel better? asked Helen.

"Oh my yes! Said Helen's mother. It was as though this thought that tormented me so, had been wiped from my memory. I have never regretted giving her that pleasure.

"Is that the only thing you felt guilty about?" Asked

Helen, eager to hear more of her mother's 'sinfulness'.

"Oh mercy no! There are hundreds of things that I could have done for people to add a little joy to their living. Countless times I shirked lending a helping hand when it could have lightened the burden. I recall the time that Mrs. Borden was taken so ill and had no one to care for her. You remember her, Helen, she was a neighbor of ours for awhile. Well she was stricken with an illness and was taken to the charity hospital. I could have taken her into my own home and given her better care and more joy than she had at the hospital. I thought about it too, that is the sad part about it. Then I decided that it would discommode our home life too much, and let someone else take the responsibility. And that's not the worst of it. I never even went up to see her, nor took her a flower. Not even as much as made an appearance. I have since, been filled with guilt."

"But mother, it wasn't your place to take her in and make her life a happy one. You had your hands full with your own family. When you were sick or had troubles, you burdened your own load," Helen said, thinking that her mother was now being too sensitive.

Helen's father smiled at his daughter understandingly. "Yes dear, that is what we all say 'I've got my own troubles.' 'Let the other guy look out for himself.' That is why we are so thoughtless for others. We say 'too bad' and let it go at that. We think that we sympathize with him, but it doesn't touch us very deeply. If it did, we would be a little more thoughtful for him, and less concerned about our own welfare. It is the little things that mean the most in the long run. You see that more clearly here."

"We think that we help others as much as possible," said

Helen. "You can't devote your whole life to shouldering other people's burdens.

"That is true," said Helen's mother. "You shouldn't shoulder their burdens; only help them to carry them. It doesn't take much effort to give a smile at the time that it will do the most good, nor say some word to an aching heart. This is what we mean by helping humanity. A little more thoughtfulness and kindness in our everyday associations. These are the things that make a life really worthwhile. I know now, that I could have scattered a little more happiness during my life time than I did. That is why I am regretful about that side of my life."

"I am beginning to understand now," said Helen. "It is the little slights and hurts, that you caused that make you feel this guilt. It is regret that you were not more of a humanitarian during your Earth life."

"Now you are getting the idea," said her father. We look back on our deeds as pitifully few, and our chance on Earth, lost."

"But most of us are in the same boat," said Helen's mother. "It is only that we do not realize our self-centeredness so that we can correct it while we are still living in our earthly body."

"Well let's not dwell on our shortcomings any longer. We have a lot of things to show you. Have you seen all that you care to, here?" Helen's father asked.

"I am enjoying it here, but I suppose there are other things just as interesting to see. It has given me an idea of the vast area covered by the planes, and also why each race prefers to have its own sphere," Helen said.

"Did you wish to see England?" Helen's mother queried.

"Not especially," said Helen. "It was just an idea. There may be other things that would be of more interest. Whatever you think best."

"There may not be much time left, and I really think that you would enjoy seeing other things more," said Helen's mother.

Helen suddenly broke into laughter. She chuckled as she told her parents the reason for her sudden mirth. "Wouldn't you just know that Uncle Henry would say a thing like that," said Helen. "I guess Uncle Henry wanted to prove what he said the other night about sending thoughts a great distance as well as close by. He just contacted my mind and said, 'My girl, aren't you through gaping around yet! Quit your sightseeing, and let us see a little of you while you are here. What in thunderation are you doing way off in China anyway. Come on back home. We have plans that include you."

Helen's parents joined in Helen's laughter as she told them of the thoughts that Uncle Henry had sent to her.

"Uncle Henry sure does enjoy life," said Helen's father. "He never misses a chance to poke a little fun. You can bet your life that he is chuckling to himself right now. Probably thinking about how surprised you were to hear his voice."

"Perhaps we had better go and see what he has up his sleeve," said Helen.

"There's no telling," Helen's mother said. "It might be that he has something that he wants to show you. But more likely than not it will be something that will give you pleasure. He is the greatest man for spreading good cheer and happiness that I have ever known."

"Well we will soon know," said Helen's father.

"I am sure glad that we are able to cover such a long distance so quickly," said Helen. "I will be spoiled by the time I go back to earth."

"You will have the memory to take back with you anyway," said her mother.

"I, that is my body, seems to be recovering rapidly, so I am afraid that I won't have much longer to be with you," Helen said.

Chapter IX

When Helen and parents entered the house, Helen was nearly knocked off her feet by the leap and bound of her little dog Trixie. He jumped up on her with enthusiasm and delight at seeing her that Helen was in a state of confusion.

"Well Trixie! Take it a little easy with your greeting! My goodness but you're excited."

Helen ruffled his hair and romped with him just as she used to. Trixie tore around the room in great excitement. He had always been a happy little dog, but now he was happier than Helen had ever seen him.

She was delighted to see Trixie too. It had been years since Trixie had died. He had been little more than a pup when he left Helen heartbroken.

Trixie barked and made a coaxing noise as if he wanted to let Helen know how glad he was to see her.

"Well Trixie, I know you are glad to see me but don't carry on so. I'll play with you, but first I want to talk to Uncle Henry," Helen said, patting him. You lie down now for awhile."

"Well this is a pleasant surprise for you," said Helen's father. "Leave it to Henry, to bring Trixie here to surprise you."

The whole family was gathered together again and Helen told them all the things she had been doing.

"I never saw such a girl to get around and investigate things," said Uncle Henry teasingly.

"I think she takes after her Uncle Henry in that way," said Helen's Uncle Frank ribbingly.

Uncle Henry seemed pleased that Frank thought so. He beamed with pride. There was nothing worse, he thought, than a person without interest in things.

He was not to be disappointed in Helen, for already she was beginning to ask questions concerning Trixie and other dogs who lived in this world.

She went over to Uncle Henry and said, "I am going to give you a great big hug for bringing Trixie here. You have made me very happy and given me one more surprise. I am beginning to think that there is no end to surprises in this world of yours."

"There are no more surprises here, than there are in your world," said Uncle Henry. Trouble is you don't seek out the things of interest and surprise on earth. You just go along in your own little circle and therefore don't know the wonders of your own world. Of course I will admit that you are handicapped a bit more on earth. We enjoy more freedom that enables us to explore more extensively, but still you pass up many opportunities that you have.

"Now for instance, do you ever take time to read about things in other Countries? No. Are you interested in things that affect the people living in New York City? No, you feel that is too detached from your life. But, do you even interest yourself in conditions existing in your own city? Such as, your welfare organization and their work, the big clinics and the type of things they do, the institutions for the insane and the research on these cases, or ever visit the experimental departments of your factories, or research labortories on the cures of human ills."

"You would find these things very interesting and educational. And you could, if you made the effort, avail yourself of these opportunities. You are interested in what lies behind things here, but on earth you just take things for granted. It should be just as interesting and full of surprises to find the whys and wherefores of the different things that take place on earth; as here.

"I guess we are, inclined to take things for granted on Earth," said Helen. "But that is because things there become so natural to us. We are used to the ways of the world and therefore our curiosity is not aroused. Where here, the complete naturalness of things in itself, arouses our curiosity. Strange when you stop to think of it," Helen said, smiling with the realization.

"Now take Trixie for instance. On Earth it was perfectly natural to have him alive and running and jumping around; but someway it surprised me when I saw him doing the same thing here. I don't know just what I thought happened to dogs and other animals when they left their Earth life.

But I never thought of Trixie as living in Heaven someway. You see that would make Heaven too natural; and for some reason or another, we on Earth are inclined to make Heaven a place that is unnatural."

"That's just the trouble," said Aunt Linda. "You try to complicate it."

Helen's grandparents said very little but were enjoying the discussion that was taking place. They knew so well the view of the people on Earth. They too had thought of Heaven as a place of Angels and St. Peter. With nothing to do but play a Harp! They smiled at the thought. How tiresome that would become year after year.

"Well," laughed Helen, "now that I have admitted my surprise at finding Trixie here, very much alive and the same, please tell me where dog Heaven is."

Helen's father laughed. "Well at the moment Trixie's Heaven seems to be right here. And his enjoyment of Heaven has been increased by your presence. If the demonstration he gave a few minutes ago is any indication."

"Well but he wasn't here when I came, so I thought perhaps he lived in a different section of Heaven," Helen said, still mystified.

"Dog Heaven is wherever the dog's master is, if he is living in this world. If there is no one here that the dog has a fondness for, then he either strikes up a friendship with someone who is living here, or lives with a group of other dogs. Most dogs like to be with people, especially if he has been a pet on Earth. Therefore he attaches himself to some person who is fond of dogs until his own master comes. Of course, if a dog was not cared for greatly by his master, then the dog would not live with him after he came to this world," Helen's father tried to explain.

"Who does Trixie live with?" Helen asked.

Trixie, hearing his name, walked over and put his forefoot up on Helen's lap and wagged his tail.

"If you would stop to think, you would know," said Helen's mother, smiling. "Next to you, who did Trixie like better than anyone else?"

Helen pondered for a moment. "Jack?"

"Why of course!" Any time that Trixie wasn't around where you were, we knew very well that he was down playing with Jack," said Helen's mother.

"Yes I suppose that Jack and Trixie still play together. It has been so many years that little Jackie died, that I had almost forgotten him. I remember how Trixie used to love to run along beside his cart. Does Jackie have a cart to play with here?" Helen asked.

There was a roar of laughter.

"Well now what's so funny?" asked Helen, bewildered by this sudden outburst.

"I swan," said Uncle Henry, "At times I don't think you have learned a thing since you've been here."

Mary, who had not entered the conversation much, except when she was spoken to directly, was now amused more than any of the others.

"According to that remark, I don't believe that Helen really knows who I am," Mary said.

"Why of course I do!" Helen said. "You are Aunt Cathie's daughter who lives out in California. It's true that I never saw you very often, but as soon as they said Mary, I knew who you were. I will confess, though, that I hadn't heard of your death; but we don't hear from your mother anymore."

"Well if that doesn't beat all!" said Uncle Henry. "Mary here is your Aunt Linda's girl. Why Cathie's Mary is still living on Earth."

"But I thought that Aunt Linda's baby died when she was just a toddler," said Helen. "Mary is a big girl." "How old are you, Mary?"

"I'm about sixteen now," replied Mary, her eyes twinkling.

Helen's father came to the rescue. It is plain to see that some things have to be cleared up. Now then, you spoke of Jackie having a cart to play with over here. We all laughed because the little Jackie that you were thinking of, is now a grown man. I'm afraid that he wouldn't be interested in playthings anymore. Just the same as Linda's little baby Mary is now a grown girl.,"

"Is this really Aunt Linda's baby?" Helen asked.

"Yes, I am Aunt Linda's baby," said Mary. "Did you think that I would always be a baby?"

"I hadn't given it much of any thought, to be honest," Helen said.

"There again, you were thinking of life here as being so much different than life on Earth. What would you think if you had a baby and it never grew up? Why, on Earth that would create quite a sensation. Well, if those infant souls that come over here weren't allowed to grow and develop, that would be quite an injustice to that soul. No they grow and learn, just as a child on Earth does," Uncle Frank said, warming to the subject.

"Mary, you are the most qualified to explain these things to Helen, for you experienced growing up in this world. Why don't you take her to the nurseries, and tell her of the different stages of your development," said Uncle Henry.

"I would like to, if Helen is interested," Mary said.

"I would enjoy it," said Helen. "But I hate to be so much bother to you all. It seems that I am forever stumbling onto something that has to be explained to me. Either I am exceptionally dumb or I just don't use my head."

"Now, Now," said Uncle Henry, "Just because I josh you a little, don't think things like that. We are all a little slow at realizing that things are not so much different here. We don't expect you to know as much about these things as we do. "Why if you did! It wouldn't speak very well for us. We had to learn the ways of this world, just as you are. Go long now and enjoy yourself."

"Are you folks coming along?" asked Helen.

"No, you and Mary go on. It will give you an opportunity

to get better acquainted. At least you will know who she is," Helen's father said, teasing his daughter about her mistake in identity.

"We'll see you later," said Mary.

"Oh Trixie you can't go," Helen said, pushing him back with her hand.

"Oh yes he can!" Called out Uncle Henry. "You can't boss him around over here. He is free to go and come whenever and wherever he pleases just as we are. Of course he wouldn't be allowed to destroy things or make a pest of himself, but he can go along with you." "Oh! I didn't know that," said Helen. "I didn't suppose that he would be permitted in the nursery."

"The children will love him," said Mary. "Heavenly dogs have no germs and they learn to behave very well."

"Come along then Trixie," Helen said.

"Did you know that Trixie used to chase the birds and squirrels when he lived on Earth?" asked Mary.

"No I never knew that," said Helen.

"Well he did. And when he first came over here to live he had to be taught that he must not molest any of the other animals. He learned quickly, however, as all animals here do. They are governed by Divine power and must abide by the laws of this land, just as we do.

"It is all so interesting to me," said Helen.

"This is the nursery for the tiny babies who die in infancy. Aren't there a lot of them?" Mary asked.

"And, aren't they sweet," said Helen. This looks like any Hospital nursery. They're not sick, are they?"

"Oh no! There is no such thing as sickness here. This is just a means of seeing that they have someone to care for them and love them. Many of them have no close relatives here. They are cared for here until they are big enough to get about. They need the association of people so that they will grow used to our ways. There is not a great deal of actual work connected with this nursery. It is more of a place for the development of the soul's personality. They are loved and cuddled and learn to respond," Mary explained.

"But supposing that the parents or some other relative lived in this world? Then would the baby be put in the nursery?" Helen asked.

"If the mother or grandmother was living in this world and they lived on one of these planes, then they would have the child with them. But of course if the parents were by any chance on the low plane, they would not be allowed to have the baby with them. A baby must be in surroundings of beauty and love. They would be hindered in their development under conditions existing on the lower planes. Many people here have their child with them on this plane," said Mary.

"They seem to be of different ages here," said Helen.

"In this nursery there are only children up to one year old. I will show you the others later," Mary said.

"Then you began your life here in this nursery?" Helen asked.

"I was here until I was a year old. Then I went to be with my grandparents for awhile. I spent part of the time with them and the rest of the time with the other children getting instructive education. We grow and develop a little faster here than do the babies of Earth. We are able to walk and talk by the time we are six months old. That is because we do not have the physical body to hamper our progress. It takes us about six months to learn to use our desires to our advantage. As soon as we learn this, we are well on our way. That is why it is important that a child remain in the nursery for at least a year. The people in charge understand the methods of developing the little soul better than those who have only recently come from earth. It is a great deal different than caring for a child in the physical body."

"You have been here for so long and were yourself brought up in these nurseries, that I should think that you would be a logical attendant," said Helen.

Mary smiled. "I am," she said. Only at the present time I am working with the larger children. Children around five to seven. We will see them before we return home."

"Look at that little tyke over there. He seems happy enough. How old about is he?" Helen asked.

"He is seven months old. Shall we go over to him? He is a nice little fellow. I have watched him progress since the day he arrived. He was only a few weeks old then, and such a little soul," Mary said.

"They walked over where the little boy was playing on

the floor. He looked up at them and smiled. Then held up a doll for them to see. "Doll," he said. "Lady."

"I can't imagine a baby his age talking," said Helen. it seems so unusual to me."

"Oh he can walk too! Come on Bobbie. Show the nice lady how big and strong you are. You want to walk, don't you?"

Mary turned to Helen from her kneeling position on the floor beside Bobbie and said, "We have to instill the desire. That is the way they progress. They can do things if they are inclined to. Once they learn this they develop very rapidly. Bobbie is just beginning to understand this, but he does very well."

Helen watched eagerly. She did not think for a moment that Bobbie was going to show off for her, but he soon got to his feet.

"There, that's the way," said Mary, hugging him tightly. Bobbie was beaming with smiles now and started to play with Mary. It was obvious that he knew her well and loved her. Mary had such a nice way with children, thought Helen.

"What is the nurse doing with that small baby over there?" Helen asked.

"Come and I will show you," said Mary. Mary approached the nurse who had the small baby. "I have a Cousin here who is visiting from earth and she is quite interested in the development of these little souls. I wonder if we could watch you teach June the use of her spiritual body?"

"I would be very glad to have you," said the nurse.

"I'd like you to meet my cousin Helen," Mary said to the nurse. "And this is Arlene, that you speak of as the nurse," said Mary, turning to Helen.

"I am not really what is generally thought of as a nurse, but I do nurse these little souls in their growth. I am teaching June here, to know how to use her hands and legs. Whether it is a spiritual body or a physical body they must learn things. Instead of developing a physical brain, they develop their spiritual mind. They must do things and see things in order to have the impression instilled in their mind," she told Helen.

"See," said Mary, "she is making this soul conscious of her hands and feet. In that way she will learn their use."

The nurse was holding the baby's hand up to her own face and was patting it against her cheek. Then she held the baby's hand and used it to brush the hair from June's forehead.

This teaches her the use of that hand," said the nurse. "Soon she will be doing it by herself. Of course these are only the first steps. As we go along her accomplishments become further advanced. I am just beginning to teach June. But you must remember that she is only a little less than two months old. Up until this time she has been acclimating herself to her surroundings."

"It is all very interesting," said Helen. "I had not thought of how necessary it was for a person to experience things and by that way learn. We are taught things so gradually throughout our life that we do not realize just how much we accumulate over the years."

"Well you see," said the nurse, "When a soul enters the physical body to begin life, he has the power within him to learn. But at that point this power has not yet begun to function. Therefore an infant sleeps, or in other words lives a rather dormant life, for the first few months of his life. It is not until he is around in his new surroundings for awhile that this power begins to come in to use. It is then that the child seems to notice people and becomes conscious of things about him. His first use of the power that he possesses is shown by crying. At first he does this by instinct as a means of self preservation. Just as the birds go south, by instinct, when the weather begins to get cold. Later the baby begins his learning, or having impressions instilled in his mind. This is when he learns that by crying he can get attention. Once he has learned this he uses it more and more. Then he comes to the stage in his development where he learns other means of attracting attention. This is when he gurgles and coos. This is all progress for a baby. And as he goes along from making his first sounds and finding use for his hands, he is storing knowledge."

"But that is only the beginning," said Mary. "Little by little as he develops his physical body, his personality is forming. That is why it is so important that he have love and understanding during his first years. That is when his character is molded. We take great pains with the little ones over here so that they will have strong souls."

"You are well rewarded with the results," said Helen, as she glanced over these happy little infants. "They certainly have blossomed under your care. It seems incredible that they gain so much knowledge so rapidly."

"It does at first," said Mary. But after while you realize that the power is there and only has to have a little help in making use of it. Souls you know, are unhampered by physical bodies. And therefore are more aware of their powers. These children will know what talents they possess; where Earth children's talents often remain buried and unknown, throughout their life time on Earth. There are advantages of being a soul brought up in this world; but there are also drawbacks."

"I don't understand what you mean," said Helen.

"No I don't suppose that you could see that an Earth life would be of much advantage to you when you come to live in this world," said the nurse. "But Mary can tell you something about that."

"I spent all but about nine months of my sixteen years here in this beautiful world. I have been very fortunate in that way to have been unencumbered by a physical body. But as time goes on I lack certain experiences that can only be had by living in the Earthly body. I find it a drawback in the rounding out of my knowledge. Earth is like a grade school. And you can no more skip those grades and go right into high school without finding yourself handicapped with children who have had the elementary training. I do not have the background of earth living, and therefore do not have the understanding or knowledge of the physical body."

"But I don't see how not having lived in the physical body could possibly have any consequence in your life here. You do not need a physical body here and so I do not see how you could feel the lack of ever having had one. I don't miss my physical body," Helen said.

"Oh I don't miss having the physical body," Mary said. "But if I had lived on earth longer I would be better able to understand things that I encounter when I am working with people of the earth. Oh there are so many times that it makes a great difference that I did not remain on earth and gain certain experiences. I do not so readily grasp the significance of Earth conditions nor the outlook of its people."

"In that case," said Helen, "why were you not allowed to remain on Earth and complete your life?"

"In my case, it was because my body was unfit to house my soul. It was sick and weak and could not function properly in that state. When it failed, my soul was brought back to the world of souls. That is not always the case though. Some souls are sent to Earth on a special mission or for a certain purpose. In that case, they are released from their physical body just as soon as that has been accomplished. As an example, we will say that a boy lives until he is only twelve years old. Now some people will say that that child had not begun to live his life. But in reality he was sent for a purpose, and also taken away for a purpose. God gives life, and also takes life from the physical body. Now if that boy taken from the Earth, created a drawing together of a group of minds, to work together for the purpose of benefitting the future of mankind, then that boy's life would not have been taken in vain. It could be either that some law was set up to protect others from such a fate, if the boy had been unlawfully killed; or perhaps that something in the medical field would be developed to prevent the occurrence of such consequence to another person.

"It is hard to say specifically just why these lives are given and then taken away. But it is done through His

Divine Wisdom to fit into the plan that he has created for the world."

"I don't know'" said Mary, "whether I have made it clear to you or not. But it is a very difficult matter to grasp. I have been taught in my life, living here as a soul, to understand God's ways and not always have to know the reason. Therefore I accept these things in very much the same way as you accept the common things of earth life."

"I don't think it is possible for a person of Earth life as I am, to comprehend fully, the reasons nor great plans of our Maker. But I do have a little different outlook on the things that happen, and can now understand that there is a purpose behind it. But a case of your kind was not like that, with a purpose. Your body just wasn't strong enough," said Helen.

"That is true," said Mary. "Had my body been capable of housing my soul, then I would have lived my earth life. But, in the long run, my leaving my Earth body so quickly did serve a purpose. Whether or not that was intended, I do not know. But Science has made great progress since that time in the knowledge of preventing infant mortality."

"You wouldn't be able to believe that, if you didn't know it was a fact, when you see all of these infants," Helen said.

"Yes we have quite a few infants here," said Mary. "But it is a very small percentage compared to the number living in Earth life."

"That is true enough when you think of it in that way," said Helen. "But there seems to be as many adults in each locality here as there is for the same area on Earth."

Mary laughed. "But you forget that these children grow into adults. Therefore, there are not so many babies at one time, but the adult population is ever growing, both through death, and the growth of our own children of soul."

Helen laughed then too. "I only learn one thing; to forget another," she said. "These things are all so simple to you, who understand it; but I seem to try to make them complicated for some reason. I guess that is because I expect things to be so different here."

"Well do you think that you understand the purpose of the nursery now?" asked Mary.

"As I understand it, it is to start the development of the soul's intellect," Helen said. "But one thing is still not quite clear to me."

"What is that?" Mary asked her.

"It is the use of this power of desire. I do not think that I really understand just how this can accomplish as much as it seems to for the soul child. You said that the desire must be instilled, through showing the child what it could do, and thereby making it desirous of doing it on its own accord. But I do not understand how the sheer desire enables him to act," said Helen.

"First," said Mary, "you are forgetting that the soul child does not have a physical body to master. He must only learn how to develop his mentality. Therefore, our first step is to develop his intellect through letting him experience certain things. That is the way we all learn, by having things impressed on our minds. We learn the simple things first, and gradually acquire more and more knowledge as we go along."

"That part seems logical and clear enough," said Helen. "For the child of Earth gains it knowledge the same way. But here, the desire, plays such an important part; where on Earth, this is not true."

"I was coming to that part," said Mary. "But I wanted to first remind you, of the lack of a physical body as a handicap. Now then, desire plays just as important part in the progress of the child on Earth, as it does here. You just have never stopped to think about it. For example; a child of Earth, after it has mastered its physical body, never accomplishes very much until he has the desire to do things. A child that has learned to creep, does not make use of his power until he has the desire to reach some object that he wants. The desire must be present, to make him act. When he desires a thing strong enough, he will make every effort to reach it. Desire is back of all actions, whether here or on Earth."

"To a certain extent, I agree," said Helen. "But I do not think that it is true in all cases. I know that I have acted lots of time without the desire to do so. In fact, I have had the desire to do just the opposite."

"That is conflicting desires," said Mary. "When we have more than one desire present, there is a battle between them and one wins out. But desire is there, and that is what makes us act. Nothing is ever done until there is a desire strong enough to make you get into action."

"Then there are circumstances that enter into the picture that have a bearing on our actions. Sometimes circumstances alter our desires. Perhaps you do not think so, but I will try to show you what I mean. You said that many times you have done things that you did not desire to do. Give me an example, and I will show you where your desire had a part in your action."

Helen thought for a moment. It was not easy to think of a good example. "Well there was the time that I was invited to a party. And as I didn't care very much for the group that was to be there, I had no desire to go. When I left the house, I would much rather have stayed home. That was my desire.

"But you must have had another desire that battled against the desire to stay home, or you would not have gone," Mary said.

"Well under the circumstances, I couldn't very well refuse," Helen said. "The Hostess was a very good friend of mine and I liked her very much. If I had not gone or accepted her invitation, she would have been hurt. And besides, it would have inconvenienced her in filling out her bridge tables. It was purely a matter of circumstances, rather than any desire on my part."

Mary couldn't refrain a smile. "Desires are very evident in the case," she said. "Only you were not conscious of them at the time. Nevertheless your conflicting desires battled it out, and the strongest desire won. Now then, you thought that your desire to remain at home and not attend the party was pretty strong. But your desire not to hurt or inconvenience your friend was a stronger desire. You wanted to keep in her good graces."

"I suppose that was the reason I did go," Helen said. I hadn't thought about that desire. But I have one that I'll bet wouldn't work out that way."

"Well tell me and let's see. I have never known a case

where desire was not behind any action, whether pleasant or otherwise," Mary said.

"Alright!" said Helen. "Here it is; Paul awakens in the morning and is tired and he has the desire to stay in bed and not go to work." Helen's eyes twinkled with delight for she was sure Mary would be stumped. "There isn't anything in the world that he would rather do than stay in bed and not have to go to the office."

This was going to be simple for Mary to explain. She had thought that Helen had really thought of a complicated case. Now Mary's eyes were sparkling with new delight. She was enjoying this debate and warmed to her subject.

"Paul's desire to not go to his office, was in reality a very weak desire, in spite of the force it seemed to have," said Mary. "This desire was on impulse, but not lasting once the other desires began to rise. Here we have conflicting desires, plus circumstances, to consider. Paul was tired and thought that he desired to stay in bed. Then the desire to hold his position cropped up. He began to think of all the work that he had to do that day and how important it was that it be done. Then the thought of how upset his boss would be, if he didn't show up, began to come to the fore. This created the desire to keep in his good graces. On top of these desires, came the desire to get his full week's pay check. Now, if he remained at home and rested as he desired to do, then he would be jeopardizing his position, as well as his chance for promotion; losing the good will of his employer, besides not receiving his full pay. These last desires became so strong that the desire to remain at home faded from his mind and put him into action."

"So far, it seems to be proving that desire is the root of

the action," said Helen. "That is, the strongest desires." "But I still think there are cases where we follow the weaker desires, and overcome the stronger desires."

"For instance?" asked Mary.

"The desire to not do a certain job," said Helen. Often I have put off a task around the house that I desired to have done. But my desire to not do it, kept me from doing it. Therefore my desires did not make me act; but rather made me inactive."

"That is because your desire was really an inactive desire. The desire not to do the task was stronger than your desire to have the task done. Therefore you reacted to the lazy desire. We sometimes call this type of desire a delayed desire. It usually comes back in a stronger form and then creates the action desired. Your desire to have this task done and out of the way and off your mind eventually becomes so strong that you finally accomplish it," Mary explained.

"Oh yes, in the long run, I do it," said Helen. But sometimes I sidestep it for quite awhile. I usually think about housecleaning for sometime before I actually get at it. I desire it done, but am reluctant to begin. I guess it is, a case of desire that puts us into action, once our desire becomes strong enough."

"In any case desire is necessary before any person acts. Nothing is accomplished on the Earth or here, until the desire is born. Take the simple act of getting oneself a drink of water when he becomes thirsty. He may delay acting to fulfill his desire to quench his thirst for some time after the desire becomes present; but in time when that desire for a drink becomes strong enough he will act on it," Mary pointed out.

"I believe that I am convinced," Helen said, smiling. I can now understand that desire is essential for the development of these infants."

"And of course," said Mary, "in the long run it is promoting their intellect. For by doing, they learn, and thus store knowledge."

"I guess I have added quite a lot to my knowledge," Helen said. "And in a nursery of all places!"

"Do you think that you are ready now to visit the second grade?" Mary asked, jokingly.

"I am ready to visit it," said Helen. "But whether or not I will be capable of getting through it, I don't know," she laughed.

They left the nursery and went to other end of the building where the children of one year to three were grouped.

"These children have learned the full use of desire," Mary said. They are now making use of it in their playtime. During this stage of their development, their mentality is developed through playing with other children. They are also taken into the outside world where they can learn new things, and become acquainted with the life they are to take part in."

"They are very advanced for their ages," said Helen. They certainly are live wires."

"Just normal children," said Mary. "A little further

advanced than children of the same age on Earth; but very much the same in other respects."

"I can see that!" Helen laughed. "What a good time they are having."

"This is their play time," Mary said. "When they leave this group, then they start their schooling. Children of this age are allowed to spend all their time with their family, if they are here."

"Oh! Then these children have no one in this life to make a home for them. If they did, then they would not remain under the supervision of these teachers," Helen said.

"It is only necessary for an infant to remain in the nursery until he is a year old. This is so that it can be taught the ways of doing things. After the first year, the child is then ready to progress in its own family surroundings. A child must however, be sent to school when he reaches the age of four. Some children even attend school at the age of three. It depends on the progress he has made, and how strong his desires have become," Mary said.

"These children seem to be progressing," said Helen, laughing. "Look at the little girl over there, showing the others how to form a circle."

"This is an entertaining place," said Mary. "But I think we had better be getting along to the school age children. There isn't so much that is unusual here. As I said, it is just play-time."

Helen was reluctant to leave. She would enjoy watching these tots the rest of the afternoon; but she knew that her time was growing short, and there were so many other things to see.

They entered a classroom where one of the boys was reading from a book aloud. The teacher smiled at them as they came in and seated themselves, to listen.

Again, Helen was surprised to see the likeness of this classroom, to that of an Earth classroom. She had not imagined that children here would learn to read.

They sat listening to the class recite. One little girl seemed shy and hesitant to read before them, but the teacher persuaded her. Once she began, she did very well, and when she finished, Helen smiled at her in approval.

Mary and Helen did not stay until the class was over, but went on to another classroom.

When they were outside, Helen said, "I had no idea that the children here would learn to read."

"They would not be fitted for their future life unless they had the basic training that the earth children have. They study reading, writing, arithmetic and language the same as any other grade school child must learn. Without this knowledge they would be unable to grasp the higher learnings. Why they even study the history of Earth life so that they can understand, the future progress."

"But it is not necessary to use these things in this life, is it?" Helen asked.

"Oh my yes!" Mary told her. "We have books to read for entertainment and knowledge. And in our work with Earth people it is necessary for us to know the things that they know and use. You will have a clearer idea of this when you have visited some of the more advanced classes."

Helen was still unconvinced of the need for such studies, but decided to wait and see if it cleared up later. She didn't want to be stubborn in her attitude.

"How do you think I learned how to talk?" Mary asked. "if I had not attended school just as the children on Earth do, I wouldn't be a very good companion for you today. Now when you speak of things, whether on financial problems, history, or your school days, I know what you are talking about. But enough of that now. I want you to visit a classroom such as you do not, have in your Earth schools. We have use for everything in the line of knowledge that Earth people do, but we also need greater knowledge in addition. That is what I will show you now."

Mary led the way. "Now these children are older and they are now ready to learn something of the ways that are distinctly of this world," Mary told Helen.

"What in the world are they doing?" Helen asked. "It looks something like an art class, but I don't see anything to work with except the canvas."

"You might call it an art class," Mary said. "But it works on a somewhat different principle. Now this girl has a picture all finished. Would you like to look at it?"

"Yes," said Helen. "Oh it is a landscape with a house in the foreground and a girl going up the path. Very nicely done."

"Is that all you notice about it?" Mary asked.

"Well I wondered what she used to paint it with," Helen said.

"Look again," Mary said.

"Oh! The girl in the picture is the girl who made it. I didn't notice at first," said Helen.

"Yes," said Mary, "And that is her home on Earth. She is learning to project pictures and does very well."

"Do you mean like projecting thoughts?" Helen asked, quite surprised by the idea.

"Exactly," said Mary. "Only this is projecting the picture. It is done in very much the same way. This girl sits before the canvas and thinks of what she wants on the canvas. As she clearly pictures this in her mind she projects it onto the canvas.'

"Is it just to learn to make pictures so that they can have them to hang on their walls?" Helen asked.

"Oh no. That is not the purpose at all. This is only a form of practice for them, so that they will learn to perfect their work. This is to be later used as a means of showing things in a more practical form to those who live on the Earth," Mary explained.

Mary could see that Helen had not gotten the idea. She asked the girl if she would like to demonstrate for Helen. The girl took a clean canvas and placed it before her.

"What would you like to have me show you?" she asked.

Helen hardly knew what to have her project onto the canvas. Then Trixie attracted her attention. She had almost forgotten that he had come along, he had been so well behaved.

"How about projecting a picture of my dog and myself?" Helen asked.

"Alright," said the girl. "But first I would like to have you both stand over here in front of me for a minute until I get the exact picture of you in my mind. Alright, now if you will stand to one side."

Helen took Trixie off to one side and waited. The girl sat in front of the canvas looking straight ahead. First to appear on the canvas was Helen, and then quickly Trixie showed beside her. It was amazing to Helen to see it done so quickly.

"It's perfect to every detail," she said. "How could you remember so exactly after seeing us for such a short time?"

"It is necessary for us to train ourselves to picture things just as they are," the girl replied. "Would you like to have me add anything to the picture?"

"Yes," said Helen. "Have Mary coming down a path to meet us."

Helen watched eagerly to see how the girl would add this to the picture. In a moment Mary was pictured on the canvas coming down the path.

"That's wonderful," said Helen. "Do you suppose that I

could do it?"

"Why don't you try?" the girl said, getting up to give Helen her place.

"I'm afraid that I will spoil it," said Helen.

"If you do I will make you another one," the girl promised.

Helen sat down before the canvas. She was nervous and almost afraid to try.

"Go on," said Mary. "Picture your own home in the background. That shouldn't be too difficult. Just picture it in your mind as it is, and decide where you want it on the canvas."

Helen looked at the canvas and mentally pictured her own home with Paul on the step. To her delight, it appeared on the canvas.

"Fine," said Mary. "Paul is perfect, but your coloring is a bit hazy on the house. Touch that up a bit and it will be fine."

"I guess I was thinking about it needing painting," Helen laughed. "I will try to bring out the color a little more. There, how is that?"

"Perfect," said Mary. "Now you not only see how it is done but have actually experienced it for yourself. It is like a thought projection, except that you picture your thought. The other day you projected your thoughts to Paul in order to comfort him. In case that you were going to remain here, you could project your picture so that he could see you. This is just one of the many uses that we have for this phenomenon.

"This is what you meant by study that was distinctly of this world," said Helen. Do you have many different phenomenons of this kind?"

"Oh a great many," said Mary. "We won't have time today to visit all the study classes. But this will give you some idea of the things that there are for the children to learn. In addition to their regular education, from the nursery through their schooling years, there is an unending opportunity for more advanced learning. Some choose one branch, and others another. It depends on their inclinations."

"I wish that we had time to visit the rest of the branches of study, but I think that we should get back to the folks soon," said Helen.

"Yes," said Mary, "Uncle Henry has some plans for later this afternoon. "They will think that I have been selfish in keeping you to myself so long."

"I certainly have enjoyed it," said Helen. It has given us a chance to become better acquainted. Back home, you had so very little to say." "That was because you knew the others so much better, and you had more things to talk about your Earth lives. My never having lived on Earth for any length of time, left me without much to say. I have had to gain my experience of Earth, sort of second-handed, through other people. But when it comes to the topic of growing up in this world, then I have had lots of experience and can add something of interest," Mary replied.

"Do you regret not having had a longer Earth life?" Helen asked.

"Oh no!" Said Mary. "After having such a wonderful life here, Earth has no appeal to me. I get enough of it just by coming into contact with it in my work. You know, I have to do a certain amount of work in your world so that I will have some experience with Earth conditions. I could only progress so far and no further, unless I understand the drawbacks that the Earth people have to contend with. By living in contact with the People and helping them in whatever way I am able, I learn to be more understanding of their shortcomings. It is only in this way that I am able to gain Earth experience that I lack. Earth is the foundation and preparing grounds for life over here. There we learn patience, hardship and sorrow. We in this world have no understanding of these things unless we get it from Earth. Our souls must have a certain understanding of these things in order to be well developed. Our scope is otherwise limited and curtailed."

"I see what you mean by getting your earth experiences second-handed," Helen said, laughing.

"Your coming here has helped me quite a little," said Mary. I have been able to learn many things from your view-points."

"I think we should be getting along now, Helen. Perhaps we can come back another time," Mary said. "Come on Trixie, if you want to go with us."

Chapter X

Mary and Helen returned home just in time to join the others in some refreshments. Helen had not realized how long it had been since she had eaten last. She had been too wrapped up in her sightseeing to think about food. Now that it was placed before her she enjoyed it, but had not felt the lack of it, as she would have on Earth in the twenty-four hours that had elapsed.

Helen thought now that she had seen pretty much of what this world had to offer and voiced this opinion.

"If you feel that way," said her father, "then there is no use for Uncle Henry to bother to take you to the medical research building."

"No," said Uncle Henry, in apparent seriousness, "I will just trot along by myself. No use to show Helen any more, she has seen all the important things."

Well now I like that!" said Helen. "You don't even give me a chance to say whether I would like to go or not. I didn't know that there was anything like that here."

They were teasing her and she knew it, but she made believe that she was taking it seriously.

"Of course if you would be interested, I'd be glad to have you tag along," said Uncle Henry.

"Don't let him fool you, Helen," said her mother. "He would be heartbroken if you didn't go. He has been planning on it all afternoon. It is his special treat for you. Although I think your father and I will tag along too."

"You can come along if you'd like," Uncle Henry said. "But let's get started. You know they won't hold up the show just for us."

As they walked along to the medical research building, Uncle Henry and Helen walked ahead of the others. "I think you will enjoy this," Uncle Henry was telling her. "It will be something different than you have witnessed up to now. And it will be very educational for you."

"What sort of things are we going to see?" Helen asked.

"You are not going to see anything; you are going to hear, Uncle Henry said. This is a lecture that we are going to. It will give you a little relaxation and at the same time give you seed for thought."

They entered a large auditorium that was pretty well filled. "This is the lecture hall for the medical students," Uncle Henry told her. "They are just about to begin, so let's get seated." The speaker stepped to the platform and the room quieted.

"Most of you gathered here today, know the reason for this session. But there are a few of you who have come to learn of our mission. I have gathered you together today for the purpose of a review of what you have been studying so diligently for some time.

"For the benefit of those who have come to be enlightened, I will tell you that these Medical students have been studying, over a long period of time, the cause and prevention of Cancer. Now they are ready to start their campaign to enlighten the Medical men in the research laboratories on Earth.

"Now then, you all know that the one task that lies ahead of you is not an easy one. Many of you have gone on this mission to Earth before, and know the obstacles that you will encounter. Man of Earth has his own theories and it is difficult to switch his thoughts along a new trend. We might say that he has the cart before the horse and then wonders why his headway is so slow. Your job is to teach him to put the horse in front of the cart, thereby getting him underway. The theory that you are to teach, you all know. But I believe that a review at this time, will bring all the points that you have learned fresh to mind."

"Now then to begin with, we know for a fact that Cancer is caused by bacteria. This is the important thing to emphasize to those on Earth who are working in the research laboratories. This thought must again, be brought foremost in their minds. Without this line of thought, they will get no place. Their other theories have left them in a stagnate state.

"It is hard to believe, that such great amount of research has been done on Earth with such a small amount of gain. That, as you all know so well, is because they have been barking up the wrong tree. "It is true, that they have, through their great efforts, been able to bring some sort of relief from the suffering of cancer. But they have not made any headway in finding either the cause nor its cure. Nor will they, until they get back on the right track of thinking in terms of bacteria.

"Now the time is right. They will now be better able to find this bacteria. For they now have in their possession a lens that is powerful enough to enable them to detect these minute carriers. It is first necessary for them to find and recognize this bacteria. It is up to each and every one of you, to do his part in helping them to see, in these tiny particles, a heretofore unknown germ. It must be found, and isolated. Only in this way, will they be able to fully understand the cause of cancer. And, until they find the cause; the remedy, and prevention of the prevalence of cancer can not hope to be checked.

"Our only possible way, of bringing this fact out into the light, so that man of Earth will understand this dread disease of cancer, is to instill in his mind this thought of bacteria. That he will then search, until he discovers and isolates it.

"In Cancer, as in any other type of disease, it is practically impossible to treat it successfully, until the bacteria that causes it, is found and studied. This was true with the typhoid germ, the strep germ, and countless others I could name. Medical men were helpless to combat these diseases, without first knowing what they were fighting. Once they were able to find the cause, the battle was half won. But in the case of cancer, they have forgotten the necessity of the first step. And though, through their many years of experience, they have found the cause of any disease to be vital, they are spending their time mostly, to create a cure for the unknown.

"We must not, however, overlook the progress that they have made, while groping in the dark. They have done exceedingly well, in view of the fact they do not know the underlying cause. They have learned to recognize cancer through its characteristics. And they have also learned that there are different types of cancer. They have found that in many cases, where they are able to remove the affected part in its entirety, that they eliminate any further growth.

"This in itself, should bear out the presence of bacteria existing. This should prove, that when every particle of bacteria is destroyed and taken from the body, that the cause has been removed. But there are many cases where the whole bacteria is not destroyed. Perhaps a very small infected area was left in the surrounding tissues. When this happens these little, but powerful germs, begin their eating away of the organs, or tissues, depending upon the locality of the cancer germ.

"Now then we come to the way that this bacteria begins to work. It does not matter in what part of the body it begins its destructive work. It only needs to find a weakened spot. In that respect it is just like any other germ. All diseases strike on easy prey, where the resistance is the least. Cancer is no exception. In the case of a skin cancer, the skin may have become broken, letting the bacteria lodge therein. If the cells, surrounding the injured spot, are strong and healthy, and the general physical condition is able to combat and kill off this germ, then the cancer bacteria is eliminated. Just as in the case of the strep germ. These germs must find a suitable lodging place where they will be free and unhindered in their work. A healthy condition is the enemy of all bacteria. This is true, in whichever part of the body Cancer may appear. Whether it is the throat, rectum, or organic regions it has found a spot that is weakened and thus begins its destruction.

"They have found that radium and X-ray treatment will kill off this bacteria. Either one is powerful enough to accomplish this end. But when this bacteria grows in such great numbers, and affects such a large area, it is difficult to keep pace with it. This tiny, but powerful germ, spreads rapidly and affects new areas, unless it is done away with in its entirety.

"We have proof of this with the cancer of the breast. When the cancer is found to exist before it has eaten deeply into the body, it can be entirely eliminated by removing every portion of the infected breast. In that way all the bacteria is removed and therefore unable to infect the surrounding cells.

"Success of this kind, is experienced with no other organ in the body. It is therefore imperative that some headway be made in the direction of a preventative of the spread of Cancer, through the means of isolating the bacteria which causes it. It is only through the discovery and understanding of this form of bacteria that Medical Science can hope to make any progress.

"These things, you students know. But the next thing is to make the men in the Medical field conscious of your knowledge. This is not going to be as simple as it sounds. You will be confronted with every type of argument against this theory. As simply as you see it; they will not. You will have to fight for every inch of ground that you gain in this direction. But you all know what a worthy cause you are working for.

"You must make them realize that there is a large family of this cancer bacteria. That has been one of the baffling things about it. In their research laboratories, they have thought at times that they were on the right track. Only to be baffled and thrown off the track by becoming confused by the different variations of the bacteria present. If they recognized these various forms as one family and studied them as a whole, they would soon be able to separate them into groups. Once this was done, they could then study the different characteristics of each. You must point this possibility out to them so that they will have something to start on. Once they get on the right track, they will be amazed at the simplicity of their progress.

"The world today is receptive for progress along these lines. This is born out with the new interest in the decay of teeth. Science has been slow in discovering its cause also. These two could well go hand in hand. We know how very much alike, the eating away of the hard surfaces of the teeth, and the eating away of the tissues of the body are. But someway, these two forms of destruction have never been compared by men of Earth. Yet it is so very evident, that the bacteria that causes each, is very much alike in character. So when this family of bacteria is isolated and understood by man on Earth, then both of these menaces will have been conquered.

"You will each be assigned to a research laboratory where you will be in constant touch with the men working there. Find the one with whom you are in complete harmony, and work with him. For his every thought against this theory of bacteria, use the knowledge that you have been taught, to be right, as your arguments. You can do a great deal through mental impressions. If it is possible for you to attract his attention to this cancer bacteria, by all means do so. You must help him to see with his own eyes, this germ that before has been overlooked. You all have been shown this bacteria on your recent visits to the Earth laboratories, during the course of your study. And so you know what to look for. Now you must in your own way, find some means of bringing it to their attention, so that they will also know what it looks like. It is spider like in shape, that is, a tiny dot with little feelers encircling it. So it should not be too hard to recognize under a powerful lens.

"You will all be expected to attend our round-table discussions from time to time, in order to compare the methods used by each of you. And to be able to further instruct you as you make progression in the Earth laboratories.

"Now then let's make this campaign unprecedented. Go out there and show that this training period has not been futile. You have all worked hard, but have a tougher job ahead of you. Good luck, and may you accomplish what you set out to do."

There was a burst of applause. The speaker had held his audience spellbound during his speech; but now the crowd was milling out.

"Oh! That was wonderful!" said Helen. "I wouldn't have wanted to miss that for anything."

Uncle Henry beamed with delight. "I kind of thought you would like it,"he said. "And you thought you had seen everything!" "That would hardly be possible," said Helen's father. "Not in the short time she has been here. But she certainly has seen a lot.

"More than some people here have seen in years," said Helen's mother.

"Do you mean that some people never go the places that I have been?" Helen asked surprised.

"Many people are not interested in world events here, any more than they were on Earth," replied Helen's mother.

"No some of the people here don't know that we have all these experimental laboratories," said Uncle Henry. "They don't get around and investigate what is going on, because they are not interested.

"Well I certainly never dreamed that they studied medicine here, where there is no sickness," Helen said.

"Every blessed thing that Earth has, was originated here," Uncle Henry told her. "If you remember that, you will grasp the great amount of work that is done here."

"Everything?" It hardly seems possible," said Helen.

"Everything," said Uncle Henry. "From the creation of souls and on up through the mechanical inventions, are first perfected here. We perfect them and then give them to Earth men."

"You said perfected. If they are perfected before we even get the idea to invent them, then why is it that we continually improve on them?" Helen asked. For instance, think of our first automobiles. They were a far cry from being perfected to begin with."

"You don't overlook a thing," said her father. "One of these times you are going to stump us with one of your questions," he laughed.

"Now that's alright," said Uncle Henry. "The more she inquires, the more she will learn."

"We will take the automobile for instance, as that is as good an example as any other that I could think of. To begin with man was used to 'old dobbin'. Now then, if he had been given the type of automobile that you have today, he would have been scared to touch it. It would have been too sudden and drastic a change for him to cope with. Why, as it was, people were afraid to ride in them. Eight to twelve miles an hour was speeding along, to the people of that time. What do you suppose their reactions would have been to a car of the modern time? Why they just wouldn't have taken to it. They had to be given a car that was suitable to their mode of living. After they became accustomed to riding along at that speed, then they were ready for a little advancement. The first cars had to be simple for another reason too. Men of that day knew very little about mechanical things and therefore had to have something to learn on. But as they learned, cars were gradually improved upon. Even today, the car is not yet perfected on Earth, as it will be. We have quite a various number of improvements perfected here that Earth has not yet taken in its stride. People on Earth are now becoming ready for these other improvements. The aeroplane progressed more rapidly than the automobile, because there arose the need for its development. The need, plus the desire, lies behind the rapidity with which these things are perfected. But as I have said, they are already perfected here, to be given to the Earth people when they are ready for them."

"Who perfects these plans?" Helen asked.

"The plan for everything, regardless of what field it is in, is first the plan of God. He then gives it to those on the higher planes to bring to the people, in whose line it falls, on the other planes. These people then study the plans, so that they thoroughly understand every detail. When they have completed their education on the perfected device, then they are ready to fulfill their mission to Earth." Uncle Henry explained.

"Then that is true in the case of the Medical research as well," said Helen. "Was the speaker tonight from one of the higher planes?"

"Yes he has been teaching the students on this plane about the cause of cancer," said Helen's father. "Now they are ready to carry out their work."

"It was as much the way he said things, as what he said. He had such a nice personality'" Helen remarked. "He spoke with such conviction, but still had a gentle manner."

"He is a very brilliant man," said Helen's mother." "The students have the greatest respect for him, and work well under his guidance."

They walked slowly along the way as they chatted. Helen had enjoyed the lecture and all that she had learned. The streets were full of people coming and going, and Helen watched them.

Suddenly she felt a change in the air. It wasn't cold, nor was it unpleasant, but it was different than it had been up to this time. She had given little thought to the weather since coming on her visit. There had been no time when she hadn't been occupied in thought on other things. Now she realized that the weather had been that of a perfect summer day. But what was this change that she felt in the air now. She couldn't quite comprehend it.

"'What is happening?" she asked of the others.

"Just a little clarifying of the air," her father told her. It is something like your rain. It cleans and purifys the atmosphere."

"It isn't like any rain I ever saw," Helen laughed. "I'm not wet."

"No you're not wet, our rain isn't the wetting kind," her father told her. "It is more like a purifier. Or you might liken it to the air-conditioning that you have on earth, although it isn't exactly the same. In the first place it isn't cold like airconditioning; but it does have the moisture and current. We are conscious that this purification is taking place, but it does not disturb our comfort in any way, as your rain does.

"I like it much better," Helen said. "I hadn't thought much about your atmosphere. And certainly had not thought about the need of rain."

"Without this rain, as you call it," said Helen's mother, there would be no flowers nor vegetation. They need the moisture given off through his purification; and we need it for the function of our bodies. We cannot breathe stale dry air, any more than you on Earth can, and remain in good condition."

"I suppose not," said Helen. "It is refreshing."

"Did you know that our air is vastly different than that of

Earth?" Uncle Henry asked.

"It seems the same to me," said Helen.

"That is because you are out of your physical body. Your physical body could not live on this air. It does not consist of the vital ingredients necessary for the functioning of the physical body," said Uncle Henry.

"Then how are we, without the physical body, able to breathe the air of Earth?" Helen asked.

"The air of Earth consists of this air, plus elements needed in addition, for the function of the physical body. In other words it is a mixture containing this air and a heavier variety which constitutes their need. But we only use the part that we require when we enter their sphere," Uncle Henry explained.

"How are we able to separate and only use the part that we need?" Helen asked.

Uncle Henry laughed. "Well my dear, both types of air are there. We just naturally breathe the only one that we are able to. The other air does not exist as far as we are concerned. Our bodies do not have the power to draw this air into our type of lungs.

"It is like sitting down to a table with a variety of foods before you. Some of them you have learned do not agree with you and so you do not partake of those particular foods. But they are there nevertheless. In the case where the food is made into a mixture, such as a stew, you perhaps lay the carrots aside.

"In the case of the air on Earth that we do not use, we do not take it to begin with," Uncle Henry tried to explain.

"I must have done just that, when I was there with Paul," said Helen. "But I didn't realize it. It is so natural to breathe that we are hardly conscious of it, either here or on Earth. I didn't know but what I was using all the elements," she laughed. "You are just too wise."

"It's a good thing that he is," said Helen's father, "with you around to make him explain.

"That's the way I learned," said Uncle Henry," by being inquisitive and a little investigation."

"Maybe if this world had the elements needed for the physical body to breathe, they would come visiting you, Helen said lightly.

"Wouldn't that be nice," said her mother.

"Well one of these days there will be closer contact between the two worlds, said Uncle Henry. "Just as soon as the people get the silly notion our of their heads that we are either super beings, or do not exist at all. The plan has been made and perfected. And as soon as the people are ready for it, it will be unfolded like all plans of the Almighty."

"Perhaps Helen would enjoy seeing something of this plan," said her mother.

"Alright!" said Uncle Henry. "Let's take her over to the training building."

"Training building?" "What is a training building?"

Helen asked.

"It is where people are instructed in the skill of communication between the two worlds," her mother explained.

Chapter XI

Helen had not had so much activity for a long time and she was thoroughly enjoying it. It amazed her that it was not necessary for her to take time out to rest. She had done nothing else much, but rest, before coming to visit her parents. Now it seemed good not to have to rest at all.

They reached the training building just in time to get in at the beginning of one of the classes.

"This will be something entirely new to you," her father said. "These men and women are learning how to produce a voice that can be heard by people on Earth."

"Well I can't for the life of me, see why they do not hear our voice as it is," said Helen. "We talk just as we always do and it sounds the same here. I hear you, and you hear me. Then why can't they hear our voice too?"

"Their ears are not attuned to the pitch of our voices," said her father. "Our physical voice box gave our tone a much lower sound than we have now, and a great deal more quality. Therefore unless the ears have either been trained, or are naturally attuned to our voices, they cannot hear us."

"But these people studying here, are learning how to make themselves temporary physical voice boxes," said Helen's mother. "In that way they will be able to make themselves heard."

"How in the world do they do that?" Helen asked.

"Come here, and watch this woman," said Uncle Henry. "But do not expect to actually see a box," he laughed. "Now then, you can see that she has before her a group of chemicals. These chemicals are the same chemicals that are found in the physical body. By taking certain of these chemicals, she is able to manufacture a physical voice tone. Watch now. She has all the chemicals she needs now mixed together. Now it produces a vaporlike form which she holds close to her own throat. This is her physical voice box."

"Will we notice a difference in the tone of her voice if she speaks now?" Helen asked.

"You be the judge of that," said Uncle Henry. "She is going to try it out now."

The woman started to speak, and Helen put her hands over her ears quickly, while the rest of them laughed at her.

"What is your conclusion?" her father asked between chuckles.

"Oh my!" said Helen. "What makes it so loud?"

"It penetrates this atmosphere," said Uncle Henry. "They have tried to create an atmosphere in this room such as Earth has, but it still is not as heavy; and therefore the sounds carry, and sound exceedingly loud to us.

"Then it is for that reason that Paul's voice did not hurt my ears," Helen said. "I was wondering why with a physical voice box her voice seemed so loud; when Paul's didn't seem unusual when we visited him. Now I can see why people on earth cannot hear us when we use the voice of our spiritual voice box. It must be very, very soft in the Earth surroundings, according to the loudness of this woman's voice when she used the chemical voice here," Helen said.

"It isn't only the loudness, but also the pitch that makes the difference," Helen's mother said. "Our voices to each other, sound the same whether we are in this world or in the Earth sphere. That is because our ears are attuned to the pitch. Our voices neither seem louder nor softer wherever we may go, as long as we are talking to our own like, that of soul."

"Then without a physical voice box, our voices cannot be heard by those on earth, unless, they just happen to be able to be attuned to our pitch of voice," said Helen. "It is entirely a matter of atmosphere and the physical body that makes this difference in sound, rather than that we speak in a different tone," Helen said trying to clarify it in her mind.

"It is just as though you were speaking over a telephone, in your normal tone of voice, and the receiver of the telephone at the other end was damaged, and therefore made your voice sound weak and far away, or not clear. The fault would not be with your voice; but with the conditions you were talking under," said Uncle Henry.

Helen laughed. "Then it is really the fault of the human ear and atmospheric conditions," said Helen. "I have experienced talking over the telephone during an electrical storm, and couldn't hear what the other person was saying due to the interference of a cracking noise."

"There you have atmospheric interference," said Helen's father.

"But that is due to a storm," said Helen. "We do not always have that condition to contend with. I should think that things would have been planned differently in the beginning, so that there would not be this difficulty now to overcome."

"Life on Earth was planned to serve its purpose. The soul was to live in the physical body under Earth conditions for a given period. And in order to be physical, it had to be made physical and live under atmospheric conditions suitable to the physical. If man of Earth had been meant to start out as a soul in his quest for knowledge, then there would be no Earth life. But that does not mean that these two worlds must remain without some means of contact. It was the great plan in the beginning to progress to this end. Humanity has been slow in this field of progression, just as it has in some other lines of development. But that is no sign that this plan has stagnated," said Helen's father.

"All you have to do for proof of that, is to look around you here," said Uncle Henry. "Why do you suppose all of these people are studying these things, if it is not to make use of them. They are in the stage now that the Medical students, at the lecture, were a short time back. But now those students have gone out on the mission for which they studied.

So will these people make use of what they are learning."

"What else do they learn to do?' Helen asked.

"This man," said Helen's mother, "is learning to make a physical hand, so that it can be seen, felt, and used, in view of Man of Earth. Later he will be able to acomplish this with his whole body. This is done by chemical process also."

"But," said Helen, "where do they get these chemicals when they want them on Earth? Do they carry their supply with them as they travel around?" she giggled.

"That isn't necessary," said her father. "Wherever they find use for these chemicals, they are available. All physical bodies contain all the needed elements to build a physical body. They can draw what is needed from those they contact, to build whatever they desire. It is mastery of a great art to accomplish such manifestation. And it requires great knowledge by those who master it. It is done only after a long period of study and complete understanding of the fundamentals."

"Of course, Helen, you understand that this is only a temporary physical body that they build around them. It is in no sense a body that they could keep and live in, on Earth again. It is merely a means of demonstration that they are unchanged by death, except, by the lack of their physical body," Helen's mother explained.

"Then what happens to this body that they have built when they have made their demonstration?" Helen asked.

"The gathered elements are then decomposed into their

original form and enter the atmosphere," Uncle Henry explained.

"Here, watch this man," said Helen's father. "He is going to make himself a complete material body. As you will see this temporary physical body is no more than a covering that he places over his spiritual body. It is like a person on Earth dressing himself in white clothing so that he may be seen on a dark rainy night; only of course in this case it is a material substance rather than just a light color. It serves the same purpose though, that the light colored clothing does to the man on Earth, as it enables this man to be seen by the physical eyes."

"Oh I see," said Helen. "Now he has himself sort of wrapped up in it. Or maybe I should say surrounding him, as it really is just placed around his own form. It doesn't change him any, but just gives him two layers of covering. It's almost like putting on a thin dress, and then putting a wool dress over it."

"Now you have the right idea," said Uncle Henry. "This outer clothing, is for the Eyes of Earth man; where the clothing he wears here, is for our eyes. It is like the picture on a film. The picture is on the film, but it cannot be seen with the eyes until it has been developed through a chemical process. Then it is only possible to see a shadowy outline until prints are made of the picture. Once the prints are made one can see clearly and distinctly all the features."

"This is just as true with the spiritual body. We as souls are like film before the print is made. But when we develop ourselves, through this chemical process, then we are like a clear print of a picture, and can be seen by the eyes of man on Earth."

"It is really quite simple and understandable, when you see how, and why, it is done," said Helen. "At first, I could neither understand the need for any different type of body covering than we have as a soul, nor how one could go about creating one. But now I understand that the spiritual body is not of a substance that the physical eye can see. That does not seem so strange when one stops to think that there are many things on Earth that the eye cannot see without the aid of a mechanical device. Such as: diminutive writing, parts of a watch, or cells of the physical body. Perhaps though, invisible writing would be a better likeness, as that also must be brought out by a chemical process. I suppose if one thought about it enough, there would be many other illustrations."

"A great many," said Helen's mother. "But as you understand it now, we will go on to the next group."

"These girls look very pretty," said Helen. "They are standing posed, as if they were having their pictures taken."

"That's what they are doing," said Uncle Henry. "They are just like any girl on Earth who is having her picture taken, they get themselves all dolled up. The vanity of you women folks is another thing that is unchanged by death," he said teasingly.

"But I didn't know that one could have his picture taken here," Helen said.

"You didn't know a lot of other things, either, about this world," said her father. "Fact is, you have never given death a great deal of thought. You are like a lot of other people on Earth in that respect. Oh, you have at times, thought about Heaven in a vague sort of way. But you imagined it to be a glorified existence of which you had no conception."

"How true that is," said Helen. "I can't say exactly what I did think Heaven was like. But it in no way had any resemblance to what I have found in the real Heaven."

"Are you in any way disappointed?" asked her mother.

"Not disappointed, just surprised," Helen said laughing as she thought about her former idea. "It is such a real life. I believe that is the most astounding thing about it. Some way, we think of an existence without our physical body as a life of fantasy, rather than just a continuation. Of course conditions are far superior under which you live here, than they are on Earth. One cannot conceive its' great beauty until he sees it. Nor can you put into words the wonder of it."

"No it is rather the feeling of this world, and the sense of freedom that is the only underlying difference," said Helen's mother. "These things must be experienced in order to grasp their significance. It is impossible to tell, of these advantages over those of Earth. It is a thing that has too vast a scope to grasp without experiencing."

"It just can't be put into words, that's right," said Uncle Henry. "But'" he laughed, "if you want your friends on Earth to have some ideas of the pleasures of living here, just tell them that if they took all the annoying things in their Earth life, and did away with them, that would be just the beginning of Heaven. To name just a few; financial problems, sickness, fatigue, politics, and work that is not to their liking. Why that alone, would seem like Heaven to most of them."

"But the difference is even greater, than just the lack of those things," said Helen. "There is a buoyancy, and such feeling of well-being that we never have while in the physical body. And then too, this world has an air of congeniality that does not exist on Earth. There is a sense of feeling unhampered in the very atmosphere. It is a distinct thing that one feels, as well as sees in this world."

"But you could not understand this fully, unless you lived here," said her father. "Like the coldness of the water in the lake. One cannot feel the sensation of its low temperature, until he immerses his body into it. Nor can he sense what this life and surroundings are actually like until he experiences it for himself."

"That is what makes it difficult to explain to one who has no conception of the great many things to be taken into consideration," said Helen's mother. "But let's continue with this subject of photography."

"Now then this also, is for Earth's benefit," said Uncle Henry. "People are not satisfied with seeing and hearing, but they want something they can keep and touch. So we give them pictures, taken by their own camera. This seems a bit more convincing to them.

"How is this done?" asked Helen.

"As you can see, the girls merely stand in front of the camera. The lens of the camera is powerful enough to take their pictures. However, they must draw some physical substances from the one who is taking the picture in order to show clearly on the finished picture. This is not like building a temporary physical body as you saw done a moment ago. The soul itself is pictured in its' spiritual body. But the one taking the picture causes a magnetic force to fall on the film. Thereby, making the film receptive to spirit body construction. For you know that the physical body is made up of heavier material and therefore is more readily imprinted upon the film. But through this magnetic current, from the body of the physical person taking the picture, the film is magnetized with a ray, like that of a light, that lets the spirit body be pictured on the film, just as the physical body is," her father explained.

"But I do not see a camera here, nor is there any physical body. How then, are these girls going to have their pictures taken?" Helen asked mystified.

"You saw picture projection demonstrated this afternoon while you were with Mary. These girls are projecting themselves to Earth rather than on a canvas picture. They are working from this classroom in order to demonstrate to the rest of the class.

"The man who has the camera on Earth is trying to develop this line of work. He now has his camera set up to take pictures. Perhaps he is taking a picture of some Earth person, in hopes that some one from here will also be on the picture when it is finished. Would you like to see?" Uncle Henry asked.

"Do you mean go to Earth and watch him?" Helen asked.

"Oh no. That isn't necessary. Haven't you experienced viewing Earth people by not leaving our sphere?" Uncle Henry asked quite shocked that this had been overlooked.

"Why no! Is that possible?" Helen asked surprised.

"Oh yes! said Helen's mother. "Didn't I make that clear to you?" We do not always go directly into the Earth sphere when we wish to contact you. Sometimes we are occupied, but wish to have a glimpse of you, or send a thought to you. This we do by desire. It may sound impossible, but let me show you."

"As you know these girls are having their pictures taken by a man on Earth. So just desire to see this man at his work. There now, have you this desire firmly fixed in your mind?"

"Yes," said Helen, "but how do I know which man and where he is?" "Oh! I see him. It's just as though I was in the room with him. He has a lady there who he is taking a picture of."

"Yes, I see her," said Helen's mother.

"You do? Oh of course, if I can see her, it stands to reason that you could do the same," Helen said feeling a little foolish over her lack of understanding. "Why I can even see these girls standing grouped around her."

Helen turned around to make sure the girls were still only a few feet from her side. What an accomplishment, she thought. "It is just like picture projection on the canvas!" Helen said.

"Now," said Uncle Henry, "if you will watch the man using the camera, you will see that this magnetic ray falls upon the camera. That is the whole secret to the success of spirit photography. Otherwise, it is no different than taking any picture."

"I see it," said Helen happily. "It is a reddish yellow glow. Quite like the red of the sunset. They don't seem to be conscious of it though."

"No. They can't see it," Helen's father told her. "Their eyes are not capable of seeing that type of light. Remember this is a magnetic light that is made from the physical body. Also, that they have electric lights on, and so causes too bright a light for this to show. This ray is more like the electricity in the physical body."

"Why surely you know what that is, Helen," said Uncle Henry. "You have it in your hair and all through your body. Haven't you ever scuffed across a rug and then touched something or someone, and felt a shock sensation?"

"Yes," replied Helen. "But I never saw it," she laughed.

"Why you have too," said her mother. At some time you must have rubbed your hands together causing a friction, or rubbed your clothing in a darkened room and seen sparks of light flash."

"Oh sure!" said Helen. "I hadn't thought of it in that way. We do have electrical current in our bodies, don't we. This is really quite simple after all."

"Everything is simple once you understand it," Uncle Henry laughed.

"There is just one thing to remember about this. And that is; that the photographer and his force are vitally important to the success of these pictures. Some people do not possess a magnetic force that is strong enough for this type of work," Helen's father explained.

"Then the soul, whose picture is being taken, does not

play such an important part in this success as does the photographer," Helen said.

"Of course he must be there, or project himself there. That is pretty important too," Helen's mother said jestingly. "Most always the soul goes directly to Earth. It is only occasionally that they use the method of picture projection in this line. This class is studying all angles of it, so therefore it is necessary for them to know both ways. They must learn all the fundamentals of this science."

"My, won't I be smart when I return to Earth life?" Helen asked in a jubilant manner. "That is if I remember being here."

"Oh you'll remember it," said Uncle Henry. "Just as you remember your life before you came."

"We might just as well get on with our tour," said Helen's father.

"Now what are we going to see?" Helen asked eagerly.

"I would suggest," said Uncle Henry, "that we visit one of the inventive work shops. What do the rest of you think?"

"I was thinking the same thing," said Helen's father. I was thinking of the little device they are working on in the other end of this building."

"That was my thought too," said Uncle Henry. "So that's what it will be."

"How about telling and me what this device is?" Helen

asked.

"Alright." "Come along and we will tell you," said her father. "It is a mechanical device that will some day be used for communication between this world and Earth."

"Impossible!" exclaimed Helen.

"Not impossible at all!" retorted Uncle Henry. "Not when it is already planned for over here, it's not impossible! And, when you see it, you won't think so either. Just when, it will be given to Earth, I cannot say exactly. But just as soon as Earth is ready for it, it will be given to some ingenious mind."

"Here is the work room," said Helen's father. "And here is the device. We call it the Spiri-phone. What man on Earth will call it, I don't know. As spirits will talk over it, we figured that a likely name for it."

"Look at all the blueprints spread out on the table," Helen said.

"That was the first step," said Uncle Henry. "Now it has taken form. Here have a look at it."

"It is about the size of a table radio," said Helen. it has dials on the front of it, but not like the radio. It looks more like meter reading dials."

"That's what they are," said her father. "This one shows how many amperes are being used. This other one is the amplifier meter. The dial in the center is the frequency dial. Then here, we have the switch to turn it on. Now I will show you the inside, and try to explain how it works.

"As you will notice, there are not so many tubes as there are in the radio. We only need a power tube, and an amplifying tube for the operation of this device. Then of course we have the speaker, just as in the radio. Now then, what makes this different than the radio, is this hollow cylinder, six inches in circumference and about eight inches in length. This is the important part of this device. It is made of a hard rubber base and is chemically treated to serve as a voice box. The chemicals are well penetrated through it, and therefore it lasts for quite some time. It is very much like a battery in this respect. This can be replaced very easily, as this cylinder slips over this extending cylinder head. It is very easy to reach and get at, as you can see. It is fastened on the end of the framework and protrudes out like a round bar. Now this hollow cylinder slips over this and when the device is turned on it revolves. I will turn it on and show you. There - now say something, and see how it works."

Helen did not understand mechanical things very well and it was not easy for her to understand completely all that her father had been telling her. She felt confused, in spite of its' simplicity in construction.

"What do I talk into?" Helen asked bewildered at how to go about it.

"You don't need to talk into anything," Uncle Henry said.

As he made this remark it came through the device, proving what he had just said.

"There now I went and spoiled it," he said. "But go ahead hear how your own voice sounds."

Helen put her hands over her ears a little to muffle the

volume of her words. When she had finished speaking, she asked them to turn it off.

"It certainly is a physical voice box alright!" she said.

"And a permanent one," said her mother. "When this is invented by man of Earth, there will be no need for us to develop temporary ones each time we wish to speak to those of Earth."

"It seems to work very well," said Helen. "But I don't just understand exactly how the chemically treated cylinder produces the voice."

"As the voice of the soul contacts this cylinder, the cylinder, treated as it is, acts as a condenser. The voice being picked up as this cylinder revolves around is then amplified to the pitch and volume that enables the Earth people to hear us," Uncle Henry explained.

"Does it leave any grooves as there is on a phonograph record?" Helen asked.

"No, there is no needle or anything that touches this cylinder as it revolves. There is nothing to cause any markings whatsoever. It is purely the case of the chemically treated cylinder picking up our voices. The rest of it functions very much like the radio. There can be no "play-back"; not as there can be with a record," Uncle Henry explained patiently.

"I don't believe that it is very clear to Helen yet," said her mother.

"Well I can see that it works out, but I don't know as I understand just how," said Helen. "But then I don't understand exactly how a radio operates either."

"Perhaps if I take it step by step it will be a little clearer to you," said Uncle Henry. "When I turn on the switch of the Spiri-phone, the power is then turned on which starts the device. The cylinder then begins to revolve. As it revolves, the voice of the spirit strikes this cylinder. This acts as a sound-board and condenser for the voice. As the voice contacts this chemically treated cylinder, it is given the quality and pitch of a physical voice. It is then sent out through the speaker by the aid of the amplifier and power tubes."

"Now then, this meter on the left of the cabinet, shows whether it is drawing too many amperes in its operation. The meter on the right, indicates the amount of amplification being used. "

"As you understand, the chemically treated cylinder, in time, loses its strength. Therefore, it is essential to have these meters to indicate when this cylinder is becoming weakened.

When this cylinder begins to use too much power, then a new cylinder should be installed. These will be available, just as are the radio tubes. This cylinder is very easily slipped over the cylinder-head. This is the essential part of the device. When this cylinder, or mechanical voice box, becomes lacking in the necessary chemicals, the result will be the same as that of a physical voice in the case where laryngitis is present."

"The dial, is the frequency dial to do away with any atmospheric interference."

"I understand it better now," said Helen.

"Of course this will be the first model," said her father. "After they have learned to understand more fully this science, then they will be given improvements."

"How will the people living here know where there is an instrument of this kind to be found on Earth?" Helen asked.

"When one of these instruments are turned on, it will send an electrical ray of light into this world, signifying its location and that it is ready to receive communication. At first only those who are friends or relatives of the owner of the device will have the privilege of speaking through it. However, as they come into more common use, then we can all enjoy this direct contact with our people on Earth. Then we will have sending stations set up here to control the air lanes. But until that time, the souls will go directly to the location of the Spiri-phone," Helen's father explained.

"I wonder if they will be invented while I live on Earth," said Helen. "Wouldn't that be wonderful to be able to talk to you everyday? I wish that I was the inventive type. But I guess if it has taken this much explaining to understand a little, I'd hardly be capable of making it actually work."

"Oh someone will invent it in time," said Helen's mother. "Then the Earth people will understand better, the continuation of life after the death of the physical body."

"Well," said Uncle Henry, "I think Helen has learned enough for one day. Let's give her a variation in entertainment."

Chapter XII

When Helen and her family left the training building, they went directly to the entertainment auditorium. There they found a large crowd already gathered. The overture had just begun as they entered, and they quickly found seats.

Helen was quite surprised to find a place of this kind. She had not given much thought to this side of life. She had been too busy exploring to give the lighter side of life much consideration. Now she was delighted to find that, they also, enjoyed good entertainment.

The music stopped and the curtain went up. Helen hadn't had time to inquire as to the type of entertainment it was to be. She settled down comfortably in her seat to enjoy whatever program was offered.

The master of ceremonies was introducing a young man who was about to sing. As the singer stepped forward with a smile and a bow, Helen gasped with surprise. He was the singer that she had heard many times on Earth and always enjoyed. His voice was clear and vibrant as always. When he finished, there was loud applause. He sang again and again before the people were satisfied to let the show go on.

This had truly been an unexpected pleasure for Helen and she showed it plainly. Her mother smiled at her in understanding.

The next attraction of the evening was a young lady. Helen did not recognize her as one she had known. She had a specialty act with her trained dogs, and it was very good.

Then came along the big event of the evening. The master of ceremonies was introducing the characters who were to take part in a comedy skit. Some of them were familiar to Helen, but others she did not know, who were to act in this capacity.

The curtain went up for the first act. Helen peered intently at those she recognized as if to detect some change in them. It was the same curiosity that caused people of Earth to expect a Star of the theater to be quite different than other people. Helen smiled to herself at this feeling of awe, of finding these people doing the same sort of thing that they did while living on Earth. It was of course, the natural thing to expect; but it did surprise Helen nevertheless.

The people in the auditorium were laughing heartily at the show. Helen was brought to attention, by their laughing. She had been preoccupied and missed the line that had caused so much mirth. Helen decided to pay more attention to the show, and think less about the actors.

Soon she too, was laughing and applauding. It was a play centering around a young actress who had just passed through death and entered Heaven. She had been used to being acclaimed upon any appearance, and therefore was demanding to see her press agent. Her bewilderment in finding the people so unresponsive to her presence, and Earth popularity, caused many amusing incidents.

Helen could see the funny side of this comedy, even though, she herself had only so recently learned the things that baffled the actress in the play.

To begin with, the actress would not be convinced that she was dead. Then in the second act she is telling her press agent, who is still living in his physical body and can't hear a word she is saying, what she thinks of his abilities, as a press agent, and fires him.

The whole comedy was so true to conditions that actually exist, that the audience doubled up with laughter. Some of them had even had the same notions, that the girl in the play had, when they first left Earth life. Now that they had learned differently, it was quite amusing.

The curtain came down on the final act, leaving the actress finally convinced of her death, and that there was no further need for a press agent.

Helen had enjoyed it, and was about to rise from her seat when the master of ceremonies announced the opening number for community singing. They were led in song by the young singer who had opened the evening's entertainment. Helen found that she knew a great many of the songs and joined in. They sang old songs, new songs, and funny songs. Some of them they sang in rounds, which added to the fun. The auditorium was divided into sections and each group began the verse at the appointed time, signified by the master of ceremonies by the wave of his arm. When it was all over, and Helen and her family were leaving, Helen spied Mary, Aunt Linda and Uncle Frank in the crowd.

"Look mother! There's Mary and the folks."

"So it is," her mother replied. "They said they were coming as soon as they attended to some other things. I'll attract their attention.

"They see us," said Uncle Henry. "They are coming over this way."

"Well," said Aunt Linda, "what did you think of the show Helen?"

"Do you suppose that they arranged this show especially for my benefit?" Helen asked lightheartedly. It struck me just as funny as it did the others. I guess that was because it hit home."

"It hits home with all of us," said her father. Without a doubt, some incident in the play hit someone. We all have peculiar ideas when we first come here that we overcome in time."

"That could very well be a true story," said Uncle Henry. "I'm not saying that it is." "It is probably exaggerated somewhat to make it funnier; but such things do happen."

"It was very entertaining anyway," said Helen. "I enjoyed it very much."

"Now how would all of you like to go home with me?" asked Aunt Linda. "Helen hasn't visited me yet. And as I understand it, she is to return to Earth sometime tomorrow. That will only leave tonight for one more get together.

"I think that would be very nice," said Helen's mother.

"Yes," said Helen, "But am I really going home tomorrow?"

"By all indications, you are," said her father.

"In that case then, we'll have to do a lot of visiting," said Helen. "Where are my grandparents? I haven't seen them since early in the day."

"They should be at my house by the time we arrive," said Aunt Linda. I also invited Jack and Margo. They are the only two friends your age that I could think of who are living here. I hope Margo will return in time. She has been traveling, but I sent her word that you were here on a short visit.

"I hadn't thought about Margo," said Helen. "I hope she comes too."

"Here we are," said Aunt Linda. "This is where I live." She opened the door and they all went in.

"Oh! This is very nice!" said Helen looking about. "And here are both of my grandparents. Have you been here long?"

"We came only a few minutes ago," said her maternal grandmother.

"So this is where you and Mary live," said Helen.

"No, I don't live here with mother," said Mary. My home is on the fifth plane, but I spend a lot of time here."

"My brother, Frank, is living with me for company until the rest of our families come here to live," said Aunt Linda.

With Mary living on the fifth plane most of the time, it makes it more pleasant for both Frank and I to make our home together."

"I didn't know that you didn't live on this plane," said Helen.

"The fact that I grew up here, is the reason," said Mary. I have lived a complete spiritual life and so have the privilege of the higher plane. But now I am learning something of Earth life, sort of living my life backwards," she laughed.

"I would like to see where you live," said Helen.

"So would the rest of us," said Aunt Linda. "But we cannot visit the higher planes until we progress to them. We hear a lot about them from Mary and the Grandparents, but have not been there."

"It is a beautiful place," said Mary. "And I wish that I could have you visit me."

"Well we won't ask you to break any laws," said Helen mischievously.

"I might sneak you into the fourth plane," said Uncle Henry jokingly. "If you didn't have the life cord, glowing from you like a spotlight, to attract attention."

"Now then," said Helen's mother, "Uncle Henry just wants you to know that he has the privilege of the fourth plane."

"Yes, and your mother wants me to tell you that she and your father also have progressed to the fourth plane but postponed their leaving this plane until after your visit," said Uncle Henry.

This banter was all in fun as they each ribbed the other one about their status.

"Things are beginning to come to light," Helen said jovially. Now let's see, Aunt Linda and Uncle Frank live on the third plane, Mother, Dad, and Uncle Henry on the fourth plane, Mary and my Grandparents on the fifth plane. Is that right?"

"That's right," said Uncle Henry. "Now that that is settled, we can go on, from there."

"Oh but it isn't settled," said Helen. "Where do I come into the picture?"

"You don't," said her father. "You are only a transient."

"Stop your teasing," said Helen's mother. You would live on this plane too, were you to remain here. Otherwise you would not have been allowed to visit here. But you must understand that each plane is made up of people whose progression varies. It stands to reason that you would not have the understanding that Aunt Linda or your father have, when you first come here to live. And so they would progress to the next plane before you would; that is, if they worked toward this progression."

"Your mother and I had head start on Linda and Frank," her father said. "That is why we are ready for the fourth plane. But Linda and Frank will soon be ready to join us."

"Oh I see," said Helen. "It is like a grade in school being divided into three groups; the very brilliant, the average, and the slow. And they each progress at the rate that they are capable."

"Or as the people in any city," said Uncle Henry. "There you find people living on different levels, in thought, and in progressiveness. Just because they live in the same locality is no reason to believe that they are of the same temperament."

"Then all the people that live on the same plane are not necessarily graded the same, or in a true sense, advanced to the same degree," Helen said.

"We are as different as day and night, although we have the same privileges," said Uncle Henry. "Just as you and the people in your neighborhood lead different sorts of lives."

"Oh mother! What is in this package that you gave me?" Helen asked, as her mother laid a package on her lap in the course of the conversation.

"Why not open it and see?" asked her father.

Helen unwrapped the package in great anticipation. She did not know that there would be a gift giving at her farewell party.

"Oh! A lovely new dress!" said Helen. "Isn't it pretty!"

"You had better go and put it on before the others arrive," said her mother. "You will want to look your best when Margo and Jack come."

"Here come in here," said Aunt Linda, leading the way.

"I'm coming too," said Mary.

"Well you women folks go get Helen all fixed up," said Uncle Henry. "Frank and I will tell the Grandparents about the show tonight.

"Well you men can talk about the show," said Helen's grandmother, "but we grandmothers must go with the others and see how Helen looks in her new dress."

Helen slipped into the dress. "I wish you had mirrors so I could see how I look," said Helen.

"Why my dear child," said her mother, "Haven't you looked at yourself since you've been here?" Here's a large mirror, come and see how nice you look."

"Why you do have mirrors!" said Helen looking into it. "I thought that you didn't because of my experience with my own mirror at home. I didn't suppose that our reflections would show in a mirror. But this one shows me clearly enough."

"Why yes," of course it does," said her mother. The mirrors on Earth are for the physical body, while our mirrors here are for the spiritual body."

"Well I'm glad to find out why I couldn't see my spiritual body in my mirror," said Helen. "That sure had me upset. This mirror looks the same."

"It is made very much the same as your mirror, only it is made from spiritual substances instead of Earthly materials," said Aunt Linda.

"The result is the same," said Helen. "And that is all that matters. This dress looks pretty nice on me, a perfect fit. The other one .... " Helen glanced at the chair where she had laid the dress she had taken off. The dress was no place to be seen.

"Why ... why.." she stammered, overcome with amazement, "what happened to it? It was there just a moment ago."

"You did not need it anymore," said Mary. "So it was removed so's not to clutter up the room. It had served its purpose."

"This one is so much prettier anyway," said Helen. "Notice how it shows off my coloring. Has my hair had these highlights ever since I came, or is it the dress?"

"Your hair has had a healthy glow to it right along," said her mother, "also your skin. But the white dress with the little touch of red binding around the neck and sleeves does set off your complexion." "I like the dress very much," said Mary. "It is so simple and tailored. It has the effect of a suit; but it isn't.

"No it is a one piece dress," said Helen. "But it looks like two. I like the looseness of the sleeves at the bottom. It dresses it up a little by having the long bell shaped sleeves, I think."

"It is very striking," said her Grandmother. "You look pretty enough now to greet a King. How did you ever manage for two whole days without looking in a mirror?" she asked laughingly.

"I've been so busy," said Helen. "I hardly would have had time, judging by the time I have spent before this one. But I can't get over the cleverness of the design of this dress."

"It is an advanced style," said her mother. "Perhaps sometime you will be wearing one like it on Earth."

"I intend to," said Helen. "That is why I am noticing all the details. I think I will have my dressmaker make me one just like it when I go back to Earth."

"And beat the stylists at their own game," said Aunt Linda.

"The only thing is, I won't be able to get such pretty material," said Helen. "This white is so soft in color. It seems to have an underlying tone of delicate pink that takes away the glaring whiteness; but still it is white. I have never seen white just exactly like this on Earth. The texture of course could never be duplicated on Earth.

"I'm glad you like it so well," said her mother.

"Oh yes, I nearly forgot to thank you for it in my excitement," said Helen.

"Don't thank me," said her mother. "I was only instrumental in getting it for you. I knew that you had spoken about having a change of garment while you were here, and I thought tonight there would be a need for it."

"Well thank you for the surprise then," said Helen. I am very grateful to the power who created it for me."

"That is enough, just being grateful," said her mother smiling. "Now if you are through primping, we will go back to the others."

"I believe that Jack just came in," said Aunt Linda, going on ahead to greet her guest.

Helen whispered to her mother, "Do you think I will remember Jack when I see him? He was just a little boy the last time I saw him."

"Oh I believe so," said her mother. "He has only grown out of his baby looks, but his features and personality are quite the same."

Helen felt a little shy as they entered the living room to meet Jack. She was afraid that they would seem like strangers and have nothing in common.

Trixie helped to break down this feeling of reserve as he bounded forward to greet her as she came into the room.

"Well Trixie! Where did you go this afternoon?" Helen said, stroking his fur.

"I am afraid," said Jack, "that I am to blame for his leaving you and Mary this afternoon. I didn't realize that he was with you until after I had called him. I was going for a swim and Trixie always likes to go with me."

"Oh that's alright," said Helen. "I understand that he is your shadow most of the time."

"Yes Trixie and I are great Pals, just as in the old days," said Jack. "Remember how he used to run along after my cart?"

"I'll say she does," said Uncle Henry. "Why only this afternoon she was asking if you still had a cart to play with."

Helen felt embarrassed by Uncle Henry's disclosure; but the rest of them seemed quite amused.

"That was before I was educated," said Helen laughing. "Now I know better".

"What do you think of this world?" Jack asked.

"I think it is wonderful," said Helen. "If it wasn't for Paul, I would see what could be done about my staying here. But, they tell me that I am to go back to Earth tomorrow."

"It's just as well too," said her father. "If she stayed here much longer, she'd soon know as much as we do, at the rate she has been investigating things."

"You never saw such an inquisitive person," Uncle Henry told Jack.

"She'd have to go some to beat you, Henry," said Jack.

"It seems to me that I have been here more than two days," said Helen. We have been constantly on the go, and seen more than seems possible in such a short time."

"That is because there was no night to interfere with your sightseeing," said Uncle Frank.

"I thought the cat had your tongue Frank," said Uncle Henry "Ever since the women folks came back to join us, you closed up like a mummy."

"Well I didn't have much chance to get a word in," said Frank.

"You know how Frank is," said Aunt Linda. "He's a better listener than he is a talker most of the time."

"The wise sit and listen," commented Helen's Grandfather with a twinkle in his eye.

"So that's why you refrain from saying much," said Helen's father. "Trying to fool us a little into thinking that you are one of the wise."

"Well you can't blame me for trying, can you?" said Grandfather.

"Here comes Margo," said Uncle Henry. "Late as usual, but hurrying along as though someone was after her."

Margo greeted them in great excitement and began to explain her delay. "I'm sorry Helen to be so late. My it's good to see you, and how nice you look," she beamed. "I have just returned from traveling. You remember how keen I was for travel when I lived on Earth. I never had the opportunity then, so have been making up for it since coming here."

Margo hardly stopped for breath. She had always been enthusiastic and had not changed a bit. Helen was delighted to be in her company again for she had always enjoyed the excitement that Margo created.

"When did you come Helen, and how long are you going to stay? This is a bit of irregularity isn't it?" Margo asked.

"Yes, I guess so," said Helen. "But I am having a wonderful time. I have been here two days and will return home tomorrow sometime."

"Oh I wish I had known'" said Margo. "There are a great many places that I would like to take you."

"I guess it will have to wait for my next and final trip," said Helen. "Mother and Dad have a few things yet to show me, and then I'm afraid my time will be up."

"Oh that's a shame," said Margo.

"Tell us, where have you been?" asked Helen.

"Where haven't I been," said Margo joyfully. In the three years that I have been here, I have done nothing but travel to all the places on Earth that I always had a hankering to see, besides visiting places here. It is wonderful to be able to travel, as we can here. My lifelong ambition was to travel. And as soon as I had the opportunity after coming into this world, I made the most of it. I have just returned from one of the planets that has physical people living on it. You know, like Earth people."

"I didn't know that there was life on any of the planets," said Helen. "Oh I have heard, that scientists often wondered as to that possibility; but I had never taken much interest in it," said Helen.

"Well there is one planet where people live just as they do on Earth," said Margo. "But Earth people couldn't live there on account of the difference in atmospheric conditions. Nor could those people live on the Earth. It was a most interesting trip through their land."

"I have heard that," said Jack. "But I have never gotten around to visit it. Are the people any different than the people from Earth?"

"Oh yes," said Margo. "They are much further advanced than the Earth people. They have very scientific minds and have progressed a great deal farther in the study of Earth, than Earth has regarding their planet."

"Is that Mars?" Helen asked.

"Yes. It is the only other planet where life exists. All the others are either too cold or too hot for human existence. These people have learned a great deal about Earth's atmosphere through instruments that they have invented, and know that they could not live on Earth's air."

"Is this planet as large as Earth?" Jack asked.

"They say it is somewhat larger," Margo replied. "They are a very peace loving people."

"Do they differ greatly from us on Earth?" Helen asked.

"Only in their body structure. Otherwise they live as the people of Earth do. These people have very short legs, compared to those of the Earth people. Their bodies, from the legs up, are longer and thus they gain a normal height. Their heads are quite a little bit larger than those of men of Earth. This difference in body construction is due to the atmosphere in which they develop. They are a very highly developed intellectual race, especially in the field of science," Margo related.

"Are they queer looking?" Helen asked, quite interested in this other world that she had not known existed.

"Oh no!" said Margo. "Not queer at all. Of course one notices the difference in their body proportions; but other than that, they are no different than the Earth people. They lead a very normal life in every respect."

"How about their language?" asked Jack.

"They have a language of their own. Just as each Country on Earth speaks a different language. Oh! I nearly forgot to tell you, they call their Country, "Homeland". That is what it means when it is translated. It was all, most interesting," said Margo. "I wish that you had time to visit it while you were here Helen."

"I would like to,"said Helen. "But I am afraid there won't be time."

"I must stop my traveling around now too," said Margo. "If I am ever going to progress to the Celestial realm. I'll never earn my ticket," she said laughing, "by traveling around for my own pleasure. But it has been fun."

"Celestial realm?" asked Helen. "Which plane is that?"

"The Celestial realm" said her mother, "is the ceiling of Heaven. By the time we transgress through the seven planes between Earth and this Celestial realm, we have acquired wisdom of a spiritul nature, and are then ready to dwell in this plane of the Celestial. It is the highest realm obtainable, in this life with out the physical body."

"Then is your work all done for the good of humanity, when you go to live in this Celestial realm?" Helen asked.

"Oh no," said her father. It is from the Celestial realm that all perfected plans for Earth and the planes originate. One living in the Celestial realm, is the one who teaches these plans to those on the planes and Earth. It is through his great wisdom, and higher understanding of the Power that rules, that enables him to carry out these perfected plans."

"Those who live in the Celestial realm," said Uncle Henry, "hold counsel with the intellectual leaders of the planes. This transgression from one place to the other is only the preparation ground. Once we have mastered the knowledge of the fundamentals of this spiritual life, we are then ready to use this knowledge for the benefit of Humanity."

"That is why I have decided to get started," said Margo. "I have practically learned nothing of these fundamentals since I came here. Of course I have learned a few things in my travel, but not nearly as much as one should in a three year period. I am practically right where I was when I first came here, as far as knowledge and understanding is concerned."

"Well Helen isn't," said Uncle Henry. "She has learned a great deal."

"Why I was here a year," said Helen's mother, "before I knew some of the things that Helen has learned already. It is merely a case of becoming interested in the phases of this life. I think it depends a lot on the individual's interests."

"That is perfectly true," said Helen's father. "Margo is a perfect example of that. Her main desire was to travel, and so she fulfilled that desire first."

"I couldn't have settled down with a great deal of interest in anything else, until I had seen something of the world's beauty spots," said Margo. "It had become almost an obsession with me while I lived on Earth. Every time I planned a trip, something happened to make it impossible for me to go. When I found myself unhampered ... well I just took advantage of it. Now I have freed myself of this longing and can settle down to some new interest."

"If you undertake other things with such enthusiasm as you have your traveling, you'll soon earn your ticket," said Uncle Henry. "It's just as well that you satisfied your traveling urge first," he laughed.

"How long a time can one spend in frivolity?" asked Helen.

"A lifetime; if he chooses," said her father. "We are not compelled to take an interest in any line of work. We can fritter our time away in any way that suits our fancy. If we choose to lie under a shade tree and bask in a life of inactivity, then that's what we would do."

"But most people seem to be active in some kind of work," said Helen.

"I think that is because it would become pretty monotonous leading an inactive life," said her mother, "especially when we are untiring."

"I supposed that each person was assigned a given type

of work to perform," said Helen.

"Oh no!" said Aunt Linda. "We only do that which we enjoy doing, and are naturally interested in. Such as the actors and the musicians were doing tonight at the show. That is the type of work that they enjoy, and so they entertain the people here. It is their chosen field, and as there is a need for entertainment, someone must fulfill that mission."

"That is the Heaven!" said Margo, "Doing whatever brings you the greatest joy".

"And your idea of Heaven was to travel," said Jack. "Helen's idea of Heaven was to be free of her ills. My idea of Heaven is to create something useful to man of Earth. We all seem to have different interests, and that is what makes this a well rounded out life."

"Are you doing inventive work?" Helen asked Jack.

"I am learning of a plan for an invention, and will be instrumental in giving it to someone on Earth. In that way I will be contributing something to Earth life, that I didn't have the opportunity to do in the short time I lived there," Jack related.

"You see now," said Uncle Henry, "why Helen has learned so much about our world since she has been here. She is a regular question box, and eager to find out what everyone is doing, and why."

"It is too bad that your time is so short," said Jack. "I could show you a lot of things that you would be interested in.

"I guess you all could," said Helen. "But I feel fortunate in being allowed this glimpse."

"You'd think this was a classroom instead of a party," said Uncle Frank. "Why don't you three young people stop being so studious and enjoy your last evening together?

"I think that would be a good idea," said Aunt Linda. "Come on now, Mary, and we will have the entertainment that we planned. "

"Helen, as you are the guest of honor, we would like to have you bring your chair to the center of the room," said Mary.

"There, that's right. Now the rest of you, know what you are to do."

"What do I do?" asked Helen.

"You just sit and look wise," said Uncle Henry.

"Who begins?" asked Helen's mother.

"I think we will let Margo begin," said Aunt Linda.

Margo rose from her chair, and walked over and stood in front of Helen. "You are to guess what I am trying to portray," she said. "I may project it in picture and I may show it by actions. Are you ready?"

"Already," said Helen.

The others laughed as Margo did her interpretation. Helen seemed quite perplexed at the idea that Margo was trying to convey. Finally she began to catch on to the idea of the game.

"Oh!" said Helen. "That must be me; as I appeared to others upon my arrival. I never would have caught on if you hadn't finally shown my life cord. I thought at first that you were imitating a star gazer," she laughed.

Jack was next. He took Trixie to the center of the room with him, and proceeded to do his stunt.

"You and Trixie when you were a little boy on Earth!" Helen exclaimed. "That was an easy one."

Uncle Henry came forward with mischievous grin. "Now then this one will stick you," he said.

Helen finally had to give up.

"Why that's when you return home, trying to make Paul believe that you have been here on this visit," said Uncle Henry.

"It's simple, after you tell me," said Helen laughing. "I thought it was someone having great difficulty in explaining, but I thought it might be someone else besides me for a change."

"Now it is someone else's turn to sit in the center of the room, FOR you missed that one," said Mary.

They played this game and many others before the evening was over, and they all enjoyed themselves. Helen was glad that Jack and Margo had come for she had enjoyed her visit with them. It would be hard to leave all these good times and return to Earth life again. But with her health restored once more, she could find joy in living on the Earth plane.

She bid her friends goodbye rather reluctantly for she knew she would not be seeing them soon again.

As she and her parents left Aunt Linda's, Helen realized that this would be her last night with her parents. She would be glad to see Paul again, but was reluctant to leave this world of beauty. Of course if she was to be physically fit again, life on Earth would be much more pleasant than it had been the past few months.

Helen was deep in her own thoughts about leaving her parents when her father interrupted. "What makes you so quiet?"

Oh I was just thinking about going home tomorrow," Helen said. "Will it really be three days tomorrow, since I left my physical body?"

"Three whole days," said her mother.
"Three days of Heaven," said Helen dreamily.

"Well we better make the most of the time left," said her father. "There is a ceremonial dance at the Indian Reservation tonight, that we thought you might like to attend. It is a beautiful ceremony and will give you a glimpse into the Indian's way of life."

"It will be the last of your sightseeing trips," said her mother.

"Well let's go then," said Helen. "I don't want to miss a thing that I can possibly crowd in. I have certainly enjoyed all that you have shown me while I've been here. As you say, it will be a pleasant memory for me. I'll not forget it, nor the time you have taken to show me your world."

"You would do the same for a guest of yours," said her mother. We have only tried to show you as much as possible in the length of time we have had."

"See the camp fires ahead," said her father. "The Indians are gathering now. It is a religious ceremony that they hold every new moon, and quite beautiful."

"It is a display of gratitude to the Divine power for the duties entrusted to them," said Helen's mother. "The Indian is very spiritual, and has a lot of force with which to carry out his work."

Chapter XIII

High on a cliff overlooking the valley the Indians had gathered, dressed in their finest array, for this ceremony of homage.

Helen and her parents sat to one side where they could watch the ceremonies without being in the way. There were a few other white people gathered also to watch this beautiful sight.

The sun was bright, although it was midnight on Earth. The camp fire was shooting flames high, as though to meet the sun. The Indians were grouping together at the edge of the cliff facing the sun. Helen watched the Indians and admired the beautiful head-dresses that they wore. The feathers were of all hues, and each one seemed distinctly different. As she watched in complete silence and Awe, an Indian raised his arms outstretched before him, as though making them ready to receive the sun to be laid upon them. The other Indians standing at the cliff's edge took this for their signal and did likewise. They raised their heads high and let the sunlight fall upon their faces. They stood in complete silence and reverence for some little time. Then they turned and walked slowly in single file toward the camp fire. Not a word was spoken.

The Indian Chief led the procession. As he reached the camp fire he threw upon it a large piece of hardened clay. This was a symbol of the Physical body that they had once lived in on Earth. They were about to begin the ceremony of casting out all evil that this physical body had brought to them.

After this clay was deep in the burning fire, he began to chant. The others chanted in unison as they waved their arms in the direction of the fire. They first turned toward the fire and then turned and faced the sun. They were ridding their souls of this evil by burning the clay and looking to the sun for the power of good.

The Indian when he lived on Earth worshiped the sun, for to him it was the symbol of the ruling power. They believed wholeheartedly in a supreme power, and that those who died, lived ever-after. It was for this reason that they feared the evil spirits of the Indian who had gone before them. While on Earth they burned fires to keep the evil spirits from their midst. Now they were destroying their own evil through the burning of the clay.

When the clay had disappeared from sight in the burning fire, the Chief gave the signal, and the Indians began circling around the fire in a dance. Now their solemness was gone, and replaced by jubilation. Their dancing became lively, and there were smiles on their faces as they danced around the fire. They chanted, and gave the Indian call as an expression of their joy.

They then turned their backs upon the fire, while the Chief covered the fire with sand. This was a symbol of burying the evil. The Chief mounted his white horse, as a symbol of elevation, and rode to the edge of the cliff. There they all turned their faces to the sun once more in a demonstration of their reverence and thankfulness to the Almighty power who ruled over them.

They feasted on the food provided for them by this Almighty one. The Chief invited their visitors to join in this part of the festivities. He bade them welcome, and placed a head-dress upon Helen's father's head. To the women he gave beads to place about their necks, and beaded bands with a feather sticking up in the back, for their heads. This gesture on the part of the Chief showed that they were now one of them, and could take part in the rest of the activities. Helen did not feel the need of food for she had so recently feasted at Aunt Linda's party. But her parents told her that it would be an insult to the Indians' hospitality to refuse.

Helen did not wish to be rude so she joined the others in the feasting. She was glad afterwards that she had, for she had the opportunity to talk to many of the Indians and learn of their customs.

They were now speaking in the English tongue, having used the Indian language only during the ceremony. Helen watched the happy faces of the little children as they scampered about with great glee.

One Indian maid who sat next to Helen was dressed all in white. Her white buckskin, or material that resembled buckskin, was fringed around the bottom and down the outer seam of the sleeves of her dress. Her moccasins were also white, trimmed with white beads. She had one white feather at the back of her head fastened onto a white beaded band. Helen could not keep her eyes off the Indian maid. She was a beautiful girl. Her dark braids fell over her chest, reaching her waistline, contrasting beautifully against the white of her dress.

There was only one other Indian dressed all in white. He was an Indian brave. He came over and spoke to the Indian seated beside Helen. The Indian maid rose and smiled at Helen as she left her side.

Helen watched these two, as did the others, as they made their way to a large rock, elevated high above the group of Indians. As they mounted the rock, they turned and faced the gathering.

All the talking ceased and there was complete silence. These two stood upon the rock facing the sun, and began their song. Their voices pealed forth through the clear air with a beautiful tone. Helen listened intently to hear all the words:

"Oh great Spirit! who governs all,
Give us strength to answer Thy call,
Fill our souls now with their need
So that your bidding we may heed.
"We praise you now, Oh Great Divine.
Pay tribute to the bright sunshine,
It's symbolic of your love,
For all on Earth and Heaven above.
"Fill us with Thy Grace, so Divine,
Help us fill our missions sublime.
Show us our pathway aglow,
Whether here, or on Earth below.
"Bless us Great Spirit, on this night,
Guide and direct us to do right.

Give us power that you bestow,
Be with us, wherever we go!"

All who had been listening now rose, faced the sun, and sang the last stanza of the song. The Indian maid and brave returned to the throng. They stood out clearly amidst the display of colors the other Indians were wearing. Helen couldn't help wondering why these two were the only ones to be wearing white. Now that the silence had been broken, and there seemed to be gala activities once more, she spoke to her parents. "This has been quite impressive. But why are the Indian maid and the young brave the only ones dressed completely in white? The others all have various colors in their dress," said Helen. "The Indian maid and brave are from a different tribe of one of the higher planes," said her mother. "They were invited here as guest singers. The Chief of this tribe feels very honored to have them in his midst, for they are the honored ones in their own tribe."

"This white clothing that they wear is symbolic of their progression. It is purely an Indian custom to designate them in this way. Each head-dress, and trimming on their clothing indicates the tribe they belong to, and their many accomplishments," said her father. Each colored feather has a special meaning to the Indian. Its location in the band, holding the feathers, also is significant. They have retained their customs of Earth, as you see."

"Indians are very spiritual," said her mother. "For they lived very close to God while on Earth. The Indian, perhaps was more aware of the Great power that rules over the world, than any other race of people in that time, or since. They engaged in ceremonial demonstrations to the all ruling power while on Earth, in very much the same manner as they are doing tonight. They used to have these various ceremonies to protect themselves from evil, and to seek the wisdom of God. Now, of course, it is in reverence and their form of worship."

"Look!" said Helen, "They are forming a big circle now, and are motioning for us to join them."

"Come on," said her father, "this is their big pow-wow."

Helen and her mother followed her father over to the group forming the circle. Helen noticed that they had built another fire and were now forming around it. She was pulled into line by the Maid in white.

"Here," said the Indian Maid, "you and your family will find room here. This is the fire of power, and we must all dance and be happy for the Great Spirit will endow us all with wisdom and power that we heretofore have never possessed."

Helen wondered if this would prove to be true. The dancing began and Helen followed suit. Soon she had caught on to the dance formation and was having as good a time as the others. She laughed and danced in regular Indian style. Almost before she realized what she was doing, she too, was flapping her hand against her mouth and letting out the Indian chant. When the dance was finished she laughed with glee. "I make a pretty good Indian," she said. "With a little more practice I'd get another feather."

"Wasn't that fun?" asked her mother. "I always enjoy these festivities". "They have one once a month," said her father. "You know the Indians kept track of time by the moon and the sun. That is why they hold this ceremony every new moon."

"The Indians are really great people," said Helen. "They have always had an understanding of the existence of the Almighty. Perhaps their customs seemed strange to the white man, but they knew how to seek the gifts of God by asking to be directed."

"The Chief is coming over to talk to us," said her father.

"I am honored to have you join us in our festivities," said the Chief. "Are you enjoying yourselves?"

"Oh yes" They said.

"And did you benefit in any way from the fire dance? You should gain some wisdom or new power when you take part in this dance. Prayers are always answered by the Great Spirit," said the Chief.

"Yes it is very beneficial," said Helen's mother.

Helen had not been conscious of it until the Chief spoke of the wisdom gained by the fire-dance; but now she realized that she too had gained by taking part in it. She had a better understanding of life and people. Now she knew that it didn't matter so much how a person did a thing, or in what form they went about it; but rather that the underlying motive was the important thing. This gave her an entirely new outlook on life, and a better understanding of people's actions. She would know now not to criticize other people's actions without knowing the underlying motive which prompted them to act accordingly. This she felt would prove to be a great asset to her when she returned to Earth life.

Helen smiled at the Chief and thanked him for a good time.

"I am glad that you could come," said the Chief. "I notice that you are still of Earth. Are you here for long?"

"I am going home tomorrow," said Helen, "Or is it today? I can't keep track of the days here."

The Chief laughed. "So it is rather confusing to you not having any darkness. Well you would get used to it in time just as we all do. Our time is not so exacting here. We do more or less what we like and when we like. The Indian people are used to that as they lived by the sun while in their Earth bodies. Of course we had to take time to rest at night while we lived on Earth, but time meant very little to us. We hunted, fished, and did our work whenever we took the fancy. I guess we had pretty much of Heaven on Earth before the white man modernized it to a faster pace. Now time is a very important thing on Earth. But perhaps it is for the best," he said pleasantly.

"I think we had better be leaving now," said Helen's mother. "It is no longer tomorrow; but today that you are to return to Earth life.

"Yes," said her father, "The Earth people have only a few more hours to sleep, and then they too, will be starting this day.

"I suppose," said the Chief, "that you have many things to talk about before your daughter leaves you. I am glad that you came for part of the festivities anyway. Come again, you are always welcome. And you, my pretty maid, tell the Earth people that the Indians still hold their pow-wows."

The Chief laughed as he bid them goodbye, and stood

watching until they were out of sight. It always pleased him to have the white people join in the festivities of his people. He had often visited the other spheres where the white people lived, but he was happier with his own tribe and spent most of his time with them.

Helen and her parents went straight to their home. Upon their arrival Helen seated herself in her parents living room and breathed in the surrounding beauty.

"I am glad to have a little time alone with you folks again," she said.

"You have been a pretty busy girl since you came," her father said. "Perhaps you would have enjoyed it more had we not shown you quite so much. It is easy to overdo it, you know, in our enthusiasm over having you with us."

"Oh no!" said Helen. "I wouldn't have wanted to miss a single thing. But we have been pretty much on the go the last two days."

"Isn't that always the way when one is entertaining company?" asked her mother. One tries to show his guest all that he can during his visit. Some times, I am afraid that we overdo it. We send our guest on his way all tired out from sightseeing."

"That's one point we don't have to worry about here," said her father. "A soul does not get tired in the same way that a physical body does. However, it might be just as well if we sit awhile and relax our minds."

"I can't help but think of how short our time is together," said Helen. "It may be a long time before we can talk like this together again. Of course I will know that you are with me from time to time, but I will miss seeing you like this and talking to you."

"Perhaps now that you understand more about us, you will receive our thoughts. That will be better than it was before you came, for now you will know that we are really with you."

"This trip is going to be of great benefit to me in more ways than one," said Helen.

"Oh did I tell you that I glanced in on Paul tonight? I was glad when I did it, that you had told me of this possibility. It makes it so simple when one is so busy," said Helen.

"Just when did you do all of this?" her father asked in mock surprise.

Helen laughed at his apparent ribbing. "Oh I'm pretty sly!" she said. "I've learned my way around pretty well. You are not the only one who can act wise now." "You're a good teacher." Helen's mother enjoyed seeing Helen and her father josh back and forth. It was just like old times when they were together on Earth. She felt reluctant to have her daughter leave, but was grateful for having had her with them for this visit.

"Supposing that you do tell us, just when did you look in on Paul. What was he doing and how was he making out?" Helen's mother asked.

"You will laugh at me if I tell you the truth," Helen said. "But I will chance it. The first time was when I first put on my new dress. I liked it so well that I wished that Paul could see me in it. I knew that he wouldn't be able to, if I went to him, so I just projected my thoughts to him and could see what he was doing. At that time he was working late at the office. Later, after the Indian Maid's song, I glanced in on him again. He was sound asleep."

"It was only natural for you to wish to show Paul your new dress. We wouldn't laugh at you for having that desire," said her mother. "You do look lovely in your new dress."

"I had intended to go with you to see Paul before the Party tonight at Aunt Linda's," said her father, "but as it turned out there was hardly time before the others arrived."

"This other way was just as well," said Helen. "He probably wouldn't have felt my presence anyway for he was so occupied with his work. I will be back with him soon now, and then I can tell him all about my visit. The next thing will be to make him believe it."

"Never try too hard to convince anyone of a thing," said her father.

"Tell them your story and let them believe what they wish. The harder you try to convince them, the more they will doubt it. A word is sufficient to the wise," he laughed.

"I guess that is true," said Helen. "Many times people will believe an untruth quicker than they will believe the truth."

"What is the old saying? Something about truth being stranger than fiction. I guess that applies in this case," said her mother.

"Well I know that I have been here and that is all that really matters. I know now where you live, and how you live. That, is enough to keep in my memory and bring me happiness as long as I live on Earth," said Helen.

Your visit will be a lasting pleasure for us too," said her father. "For we will know that you no longer think of us as dead; but living a normal well rounded out life."

"There is just one thing that I wanted to see before I went back to Earth," said Helen. "That there won't be time for; that will be my one regret."

"What is that?" her father asked perplexed.

Helen smiled a little, for she didn't want them to think her ungrateful for all they had shown her. She had seen many things of much more importance to round out her understanding, than simply to see the way their churches were conducted. But someway it seemed to leave something lacking in her knowledge.

"Come, come, girl," "Don't sit there acting as though you were afraid to speak up," said her father. "Maybe there is still time. We had one more thing planned for you, but if there is something else you would rather do?"

"Well," said Helen hesitatingly, "It was just that I wanted to see what sort of a sermon they preached over here. Are they different, I mean the type of service?"

Helen's parents sighed with relief. They had been afraid that their daughter was to return to Earth disappointed.

"We had already made plans to attend church this morning," said her mother. "You will not be going back to your Earth body until early afternoon. Paul will be at the hospital when you return to Earth and the Doctor will be there also. It has been timed for the convenience of all."

"The stage all set, waiting for the star to appear," said Helen jestingly. "I guess I'll really give them a show. That is if I feel as well as I do now. How will I feel when I go back into my body?"

"You should feel pretty well," said her mother. "Your body has had a rest and is now getting back in perfect order. When the blood clot has thoroughly dissolved, which it will have by this afternoon, your body will be functioning perfectly again. Your soul has been free and gained strength from the Divine power. So I know of no reason why you would not be able to put on as big a show as you wish."

"What sort of a show are you talking about," asked her father.

Helen chuckled. "Oh I was just wondering what they would say, if I rallied and told them some of the things they had been doing, while I apparently slept. Or, suddenly set up and told the Doctor that the blood clot was gone, and I wanted to get out of the hospital."

"They'd probably put you in a straight jacket'; or under ether," said her father chuckling at the thought of Helen doing such a thing.

"You wait and see," said Helen mischievously. "I'll show them that I know what's been going on. They may think that I am still delirious, or slightly irrational, but when they find out that what I say is true"

"You would sure have them worried," said her father, laughing at the very thought of it. They'd be afraid you'd have a relapse by going home so soon after coming out of your coma."

"Is there any chance that I would?" Helen asked sobering.

"No, none at all. You would not be allowed to return to your body in that case," said her father.

"Well then," said Helen, "I will certainly see to it that they don't keep me confined to my bed in the hospital very long."

"It will be just as well to remain peacefully for the night. They wouldn't under any circumstances release you from the hospital before morning. They would consider it too great a risk," said her mother. "And your body will seem a little weak at first because of lying in bed without use, but by morning it will have gained strength by your use of it."

"You needn't be afraid to move about, for you can cause no harm. They will warn you against moving about too much, for fear that you would cause the blood clot to start moving in the wrong direction. But as there will be no blood clot, it will only tend to strengthen your body," said her father.

"It will seem a little strange to think of there being two of me," said Helen. "I often forget about the physical body that is in the hospital. It is like taking off an old dress and putting on a new one; the old one is forgotten. It is like this dress and the one I had on earlier in the day. The other one is of no further use to me anymore, but this one now serves me well. It is like the physical body serving its purpose while I lived on Earth, and this body serving my needs for this life. Off with the old and on with the new, could very well be the definition of Death," Helen said flippantly.

"But instead, it causes unnecessary mourning," said her mother. "Can you imagine someone grieving over someone's good fortune," her mother said smiling. "Yet that is just what people do.

"That is because we don't understand," said Helen. "Fact is, I am beginning to feel a little regretful that I am going to leave you. One might say that I was dying by going back to my physical body. It is really just the same as leaving the physical body, because by this change of bodies we live with different people and therefore miss being with them in the same way.

"We will miss having you with us too," said her mother. "In a sense, you are dying from this world, for you will no longer have an active part here. That is true when one leaves Earth and comes here, and it is just as true in your case."

"It is like moving away and leaving your friends," said Helen. "But soon one makes new friends and goes on living just the same. At first one's friends dislike to have one leave; but when they get used to your being away and know that you like your new location, they may miss you; but they do not grieve."

"Yes but people do not think of death that way," said her father. "If they did, it would be better for all concerned." "It is just the same as moving to a distant place where you do not see your friends or family for years. But of course they know that they are living on Earth some place, and that seems to make a difference in the attitude they take. The fact that they never hear from them throughout the years does not grieve them greatly."

"It's really just a difference in thinking," said Helen.

"That's all," said her mother. "If people thought of death as a move for the betterment of the person, they would rejoice for them instead of sorrowing."

"Each person has a different interpretation," said Helen. "Think of all the religious beliefs that there are. By the way, which religion is the right one?

"That depends on what you term religion," said her mother smiling.

"Living our lives as best we can each day with the knowledge that God is master of our souls, is the basis for true religion. Our conduct and purity of thoughts in our everyday life represents our only claim to the right to profess that we have any religion. The right religion, is living up to a high standard, set by ourselves, to bring as much good to the world as a whole, that we are capable of creating. The way we go about giving reverence is not as important, as the feeling with which we offer it. So it is really a case of each individual's religious manifestations, rather than that of the Church as a whole."

"You see," said Helen's father, "it is not so important by what name we call our form of worship, as it is that we live up to it. It is possible to attend church services without having any love in our hearts for our Maker. This is in no sense paying tribute to our Heavenly Father."

"But each church believes differently," said Helen.

"It is merely a difference in interpretation of the Bible," said her mother. "They all believe the same fundamental truth concerning God, and Jesus and revere them. The variations in interpretation is not so important. They all have the same basic knowledge of a Divine Power, and this is the important thing. The way that each goes about worshiping, holds little significance in effecting the rightness of that religion. All are fundamentally right."

"You saw that tonight, clearly, by the demonstrations of the Indians. That was their form of worship, and I am sure that the Great Spirit understood what was in their hearts," said her father. "It is not so much what we do; but what we feel, when we worship. So the denomination is of no real importance," said her father.

"If it were, we wouldn't have all the denominations of the churches here," said her mother.

"Don't tell me that you are still a Methodist!" exclaimed Helen.

"We still attend the Methodist church regularly," said her mother. "It was only natural for us to seek our own church when we came here to live. Just as in any City that we might have moved to on Earth. People like to continue on with things they are used to, and that is just as true in regard to the church. We have Catholic, Protestant, Jew, Hindu, Indian, and a great many other forms of religion here. Each carries out his worship in the manner that he was accustomed to while living on Earth."

"Then it's not the way, we worship that counts, but the

thought behind it," said Helen. "I'm glad to know that. Let each worship as he sees fit, and see that you live to the best of your ability, would be a very good motto then."

"Mottos like that are pretty hard to live up to some times," said her father with a chuckle. "Watch yourself when you return to Earth and see how many times you take a critical attitude. I'm afraid that it would surprise you if you kept count. However, it seems to be Human nature to want to live the other fellow's life for him. It is difficult enough to try to make one's own life a thing of worthwhile without bothering about the faults of another."

"I'd like a drink of water," said Helen. "I guess I have talked too much," she laughed.

"Come and have a drink; and then we had better be going to church. The time is going right along," said her mother.

"Yes, and my visit will soon come to an end," said Helen.

"But someday you will join us again and take up where you left off," said her mother. "We will have many things of interest to show you then, that we have discovered during your absence."

"Come on Helen, stop looking at yourself in the mirror. You look alright. We must be going to church or it will have started," said her father.

Chapter XIV

The church had nearly filled when Helen and her parents took their places. Helen looked around in admiration of the beauty of the church. The organ music filled the room, and the choir was in readiness.

It seemed to Helen quite like any church on Earth. The people were nodding to their friends as they passed by and occasionally stopping for a word.

Now all the people seemed to have settled down, and the whispering had stopped.

The minister approached the pulpit and announced the first song. A rustle went over the room as everyone turned to the page of the song. The choir rose, and the congregation did likewise. Helen couldn't refrain a smile as she stood up to sing. Everything was so normal, that it amused her. If it were not being with her parents, she could easily believe that she was in her own church on Earth. Except for the feeling of serenity that she sensed hovering in the atmosphere, and the outstanding beauty of the church, everything seemed to be conducted in the same way.

There were several songs by the congregation, and then two songs sung by the choir. Helen listened to the beauty of their voices.

When the last number was finished, the minister rose from his chair and stepped forward.

"We have gathered here today, in reverence to our Almighty God. Also, to learn more about the ways of our Creator. We are all fortunate in living so close to Him in our daily lives. But many of us are still wanting for some enlightenment."

"Today I have taken for my subject, 'God's Children'. We are all, without exception, his children. To believe otherwise, would be contradicting the teachings of Jesus, who was given to the world as God's first messenger, that there was a Heavenly Father, and that we were all his children."

"We are all familiar with the scripture, 'For God so loved the world, that He gave His only begotten son, that whosoever believeth in him should not perish but have everlasting life!" But many of us do not understand the meaning of these words. We are apt to take this to mean that Jesus was God's only, only, son. And that he was different from the rest of God's children. This however is not true. The soul of Jesus was placed in the physical body, just as was our own soul, placed in our physical body. Jesus was a gifted soul, sent on a special mission to fill; just as other souls have been sent from time to Time in different fields."

"We are apt to think of Jesus as a Divine soul, because of his powers that he possessed while living on the Earth. He was born with an insight and understanding of this great world in which we now live. He saw visions that helped him overcome many obstacles that fell in his pathway. He lived close to God in his infinite Grace, and thereby was directed in the way he was to go."

"Perhaps some of you have the belief that Jesus was sacrificed on this mission to Earth. That God gave up his, only, son that man on Earth would know of the life to follow. Jesus was loaned to Earth, as are all of God's children. That they bring into the world some new truth."

"Some are carpenters who in some way help to develop new things for the progress of the world. Others are great inventive geniuses who promote advancement for the Earth people. There are innumerable fields for these souls of God to enter. Each individual soul is sent to Earth to fill a niche, either doing small things or great things."

"But God is not sacrificing His children by giving them to Earth, for it is His intention that they shall dwell on Earth for a given time and each fill his mission."

"Jesus was a soul filled with compassion for all men on Earth. Many were the times that Jesus was confronted with the same temptations and hardships that we all were. But Jesus was so filled with the wisdom of malice towards none, that he retaliated with kindness and love. It was his hope that by showing the spirit of brotherhood, that those who listened to his teachings would heed his words."

"But Jesus was scoffed at, and mistreated for his kindly deeds. It was only after years, that his teachings, and mission to Earth was recognized for its greatness. Time was the benefactor of his miraculous accomplishments. Lost seemed his mission to Earth when he was crucified; but God knew well what this child of Earth had accomplished in a few short years."

"Jesus had been a sower of seeds, that were to flourish and bloom as the years went on. To have held Jesus in his physical body would not have served God's great plan so well; as to let Jesus be crucified. For through the death of the physical body of Jesus, his teachings were proven. Jesus was loaned to Earth, that through his crucifixion, those who scoffed and disbelieved his teachings would be convinced that life did not end with the death of the Physical; but was everlasting."

"When Jesus arose, from the so-called dead, and showed himself to those with whom he lived on Earth, his mission proved not in vain."

"He, like all of us, then came to dwell in this world of souls. Jesus as you all know did not, as supposed by the Earth people, come here to be praised for his mission to Earth. He, like others, came here to go on doing the bidding of God. Since coming here to live on, as a soul without the physical body, Jesus has continued his healing and comforting to those who suffer on Earth.

"We see him often in our daily lives, mingling with the other souls. He has not stopped his labors for the good of humanity. Oh no! Without the physical handicaps to hamper him, and living closely with God, he is carrying on the great mission begun in Earth life."

"Today we have many great leaders living in this world of souls. Leaders, who are also commemorated by the Earth people, because they too, filled an outstanding mission on Earth."

"Some of us, were but the power that helped to turn the wheels of Earth life, while we lived in our physical bodies. But that is no reason, that we also, are not God's children. Oh no, for we had our small part to play. Although it may not have been as outstanding a part as some others have taken, still our lives on Earth were for a purpose."

"Just as each of you, here, fill a place laid out for you in God's great plan."

"Is it then not to be expected, and understood, that we too are God's children? For were we not given the same type of physical body, and the same chance on Earth that Jesus was? And were we not also taken to our Heavenly home with the death of that physical body? Of course we were, for we also are God's own children."

"God has no favorite son, nor did he plan to have. We are each one important in God's great plan, whether our mission be great or small. Just as each child has a place in its mother's heart."

"We did not die with the death of our physical body, even though we may not all, have lived by the teachings of Jesus. For God never intended to shut the door on any of His children."

"Jesus said, 'That whosoever believeth in him should not perish but have everlasting life.' By that Jesus did not intend to imply that those who did not believe his teachings, would not, enter the Kingdom of Heaven. Jesus only wanted the world to know that life existed after the death of the physical body. And all who believed his teachings would know of this wonderful life of souls, and therefore not fear the death of the physical, that would some day come to them all."

"Love thy neighbor, Jesus said. Did he actually mean this statement to be taken literally? No. He meant that we would be kind and considerate, and befriend all of those with whom we came in contact."

"Jesus lived what he taught. He gave not an unkind thought, or act, to those who tormented him. Even when he was crucified, he said, 'Forgive them, Father, for they know not what they do.' Yes, Jesus was a soul of gentility and love. That is why we are so apt to look upon him as a favored son of God. But we have only to stop and think of other great souls who have also lived on Earth and suffered for their cause."

"Abraham Lincoln was a great soul on a special mission to Earth. He was also, a kind, gentle, humane man; but he also faced many trials and tribulations during his Earth life. He also lost his life on Earth, by one who cared not for his teachings. Today we find Lincoln commemorated by the Earth people for fulfilling his mission so ably. Not reverened, perhaps, in the same way as Jesus; but commemorated for the principle that he, lived and died for."

"There are hundreds upon hundreds of souls, who I could name, who have filled great missions on Earth, just as Jesus did, only in different fields."

"Will there be another Jesus sent to Earth? Another Lincoln, Beethoven, Mozart, Shakespeare, and the many inventive geniuses who have filled missions on Earth? No, not souls who will be known by these names. But there will be other souls to fill the many fields that these once filled so ably. Each generation will be sent a certain number of souls who will reach greatness, and a certain number of souls who will help in the progress of the world. These will not take the places of whose who have filled their mission on Earth; but rather will carry on from where these have left off. As time goes on, the need changes. Jesus planted the seeds for religion, and others are carrying on that these seeds will not perish. Lincoln was a leader for his time. He was inspired by Divine power for the good of humanity. So others who follow, will also fill their mission through Divine guidance. For God created the world and the children He puts in it. He gives and He takes away, for the good of his unfolding plan."

"You here today, know now, what your missions were on Earth, and know how well you filled them. You are also now going on and in some way helping in God's great plan."

"Forever and ever, God's children will be sent to Earth on missions. Some will be planters of seeds, others will be the cultivators; some will reap the harvest, others will help in pulling the load; all are God's children."

"No matter how small, or seemingly unimportant a part we take in life, we serve our purpose. For it takes a multitude of people to make a world. And a multitude of missions are yet to be fulfilled before the Great plans of God are all unfolded to the Earth people."

"We here, have a great work to do in the unfoldment of these plans. We are living in a world where we are unhampered and have full knowledge of our tasks. We are not working in the dark, as we were while in our physical bodies. We have but to ask, and the way is shown to us, whereby we can progress in our chosen missions."

"Then is it any wonder that I say, that we are all God's children? Do you not feel His love and wisdom with you wherever you go? Does He not tell you by voice, and guide you on your pathway? You are instructed now, just as Jesus was while on Earth. Can you not see then, how Jesus was so capable while in his physical body? Living in close contact with God, while Jesus lived on Earth, is the answer to the powers and wisdom that Jesus possessed. These same powers are now within our reach, for we live with God and feel his presence wherever we are."

"If there are some among you who have not learned yet of the powers you possess as a soul, by all means seek this wisdom, either in the Cathedral or in the quiet of your home. Your quest for this knowledge, of the powers that you have in your possession, will be given to you. But you must seek.. Nothing comes to those who want not. For only through your desire, does God feed your soul with knowledge. If you show no interest in His great plan for you, or that of the world, then how can you expect Him to shower His blessings upon you. Seek and you shall find the gifts given to you."

"Jesus, while living in the physical body, had the thirst for more knowledge, and so he sought God's wisdom. God only planted the seeds within the soul of Jesus, of the great truths for his teachings. Jesus nourished those seeds, and they grew and unfolded into a great understanding of the powers of God. By asking for knowledge and guidance, and following the pathway that God had laid out before him, Jesus was filled with the Divine power. That was the secret of the success and greatness of Jesus."

"We all had seeds of some kind planted in our souls while we lived on Earth. Some of us made those seeds flourish and bloom; while others let the seeds remain buried in darkness. These seeds regardless of kind, must be brought to light in order to grow and unfold in whatever field they may be in."

"So you today, who still have not uncovered the seeds of gifts, that lie deep in your soul, seek them out and bring them into the light under the power of God, and begin to fulfill your mission whatever it might be."

"God does not say, you must do this, or you must do that. He is a loving Father who waits for his children to seek His guidance. Jesus in his great wisdom of today, is ever seeking the counsel of God. He began early in Earth life the quest for the Almighty's knowledge. That is why he was so enlightened while he lived as a man of Earth. His seeds were harvested. Now he is continually planting, and reaping new yields. He has learned the way of conquest. You also have these opportunities. All paths are open to you, just as they are to Jesus."

"When I meet Jesus, around on the different planes, and see his radiant countenance, I look upon him in reverence for the great work he is doing. He fills my soul with new eagerness to do a greater work for my Father. Jesus is far advanced in this beautiful world and is filled with great wisdom. Just because he dwells in the celestial realms, does not keep him from going on with his chosen work among us."

"We could well pattern our lives after Jesus. Just because we have attained a level of beauty, and find life so satisfying, is no reason to come to a standstill in our missions."

"Jesus was far more advanced in this life when he came here from Earth, than we are. But did he content himself to bask in the Glories of God? No- Jesus was possessed with the desire to continue on with his mission, bringing understanding and comfort to all people. The very fact that he was rewarded with such Glories, as being worshiped by the Earth people, prompted him to make himself worthy of their love. He so greatly appreciated the opportunities given to him that he set out to be worthy of their praises. He felt that such praise was not justly forthcoming for his meager deeds while on Earth. So he took it upon himself to do a greater work for God who had given him so many blessings. Today, he is still going on, progressing farther and farther, and doing more and more, so that his followers will have no regrets nor disappointment in their faith in him."

"Of course this life seems pretty wonderful for us after Earth life, and for awhile we all, feel, that we just want to bask in the Glory of it. But there are things that we each can do in thankfulness for this wonderful life we are allowed to enjoy."

"Seek out your field, of contribution in this great unfoldment of beauty and splendor. Let your soul go on in its progression by finding something worthwhile to do. Whether it be bringing joy to someone, or in some creative work; but seek the wisdom of God, and then do his bidding unrelentlessly, as Jesus is doing."

"Let us pray: Our Father, creator of all souls, without distinction between us, we have gathered here today to be filled with Thy wisdom. We are thankful for your presence here today, and for the beauty of the radiance that floods our church. Fill our souls with light, that all seeds will grow into deeds of worth. Promote our aims with your wisdom, and keep us ever going on in the footsteps of Jesus. Let us be filled with Thy wisdom, that we may also fill our lives with some worthy mission, in return for all the wondrous gifts you have bestowed upon us."

"With malice towards none, and love for all of humanity in our hearts we are thankful for our many blessings. Amen."

"Let us all rise and sing, 'Glory be to our Father'."

The congregation arose and sang.

Helen looked about and saw the radiant light that filled the room as the people sang their praise. It seemed to grow brighter with each word of the song. As Helen sang, her soul seemed to be uplifted by the power of God's presence. She had never experienced anything quite like it. It was as though a million sparks had ignited in her soul and flooded it with a radiant light. The glow that she felt within her, filled her with a spontaneous power of knowledge, of the mission which she was to fill when she returned to Earth. She, too, must be a scatterer of seeds of the truth of this world, that she had been so privileged to visit. Before she had time to recover from this unexpected knowledge, the minister had given the benediction, and the people were leaving their seats.

"The service is over," said Helen's mother tapping her on the arm.

Helen had been deep in thought and was hardly aware of the voices about her. She rose from the seat and followed her parents to the outer hallway. There Helen met several of her parents' friends. They stood chatting there when the minister came over and greeted them.

"Good morning," he said. "This must be your daughter. I

have heard that she is visiting you from Earth."

"Yes, this is our daughter Helen," said Helen's father smiling proudly. "Her visit is about over. She is returning to Earth life today, probably in an hour or so."

Helen nodded and spoke to the minister. "I enjoyed the service," she said.

"I am glad that you could be here," said the minister. Our sermons vary a little from those of Earth. Our teachings are more on the use of the soul and how to best make our lives more useful. We are constantly having newcomers, and therefore arrange our sermons to fit the need. It is a wonderful life, but one must know how to go about making it a life of usefulness as well as one of enjoyment."

"I was a bit surprised," said Helen, "to learn just how important a part we all have in the world. I had never thought of life in exactly that way. But as you pointed out, each generation has its outstanding people in all fields. The rest of us are more or less their supporters."

"We all go in to making up a well balanced world," said the minister. "Each person on Earth contributes something to his world, just as each person fills a need. Our world needs people in all fields of this life in order to make it a normal world of progression. Our life here, and the stride we make, reflects on the progress of your world. Did you know that?"

"I realize that more and more since this service." said Helen.

Helen's parents looked at her, not understanding the

exact meaning of her remark. They wondered just how this service had accomplished this understanding, more than all the other examples of this fact.

"I am sorry that you will not be here to attend more of our services," said the minister. "You would learn many things of value to you in your Earth life. I can say that without hesitation, for I am not always the speaker," he said jovially.

Helen laughed. "You are too modest. I think you were very good."

"Thank you," said the minister. "But we have some who are far more learned, that I wish you could hear."

"Well if we don't get along, she may have that opportunity," said her mother smiling. "I don't think we can keep her much longer out on the leash of her life cord without its losing its power."

"To hear them talk about my life cord you'd think I really had a cord dangling after me," said Helen, "instead of just a glowing ray. They tease me unmercifully about it," said Helen. "What do you think I ought to do to them?"

"Ignore them," said the minister good naturedly. "They are only jealous because they were never allowed to carry one. It is really quite a distinction and you should feel very proud."

"I guess that is it," said Helen's father," looking at her mother. "But I think we had, better be leaving before it goes out," he still teased.

They bid their friends and minister goodbye in a jovial spirit, and promised to tell them whether the life cord held out, the next time they saw them.

When they were out on the street, Helen's mother said, "What took you off into a dream world at the last of the service?"

"The most amazing thing happened while we were singing the last song," said Helen. "I was watching the beautiful rays of light that flooded the church, when all of a sudden I felt a warm glow pass over me. It was like the warm rays of the sun penetrating deep inside of me. Then suddenly it was like a voice speaking into my ear, and it said, 'Scatter the seeds of the truth of what you have learned while on this visit. Your mission will be thus fulfilled by entering this field of work. You will be the planter who sows the seeds of enlightenment of this beautiful world of souls. Drop them wherever you go, that others may nourish them until they blossom throughout the whole Earth world. You will be guided along this pathway and be given wisdom with which to fulfill this mission."

"I was so stunned by this experience that I was carried away for a moment. It was the most wonderful experience that I have ever had."

"That is what the minister was talking about today when he said seek out your rightful field of work," said her mother. "You must have been wondering what your field was, in order to have been inspired by the power of God. That is what we mean when we say that we hear the voice of God, directing us. Just as the man on the low plane was told the way he must go, at the Cathedral that day. He sought the wisdom of God, and was shown the way of recompense."

"I am thankful to have had such an experience," said Helen. "It made me fully understand the powers of God, who plans all our lives, both here and on Earth, to serve His purpose. All things done here are primarily to benefit those who live on Earth. The people here learn of God's plans first, and are then able to work them out in preparation for the Earth. All teachings, regardless of what field they may be in, seem to originate here.

"That is true," said her father. "God creates man and everything that he possesses."

"We can take very little credit then, for all of our progress on Earth," said Helen. "Very few, if any, of the people on Earth are conscious of this well formed plan for our progress. We do not realize that we are puppets, moved in our actions by this supreme power."

"Perhaps you cannot take all the credit," said her father," but after all, if you fill your mission well, then some of the credit is due for carrying out the original plan. Doing the best possible under the circumstances which confront one, is the most to be expected. Plans are laid pretty well, and most people fulfill their mission in part, if not all. Sometimes people are slow in finding their field of work, and often do not enter it when first becoming conscious of their leaning towards it. But eventually, it usually works out as planned by our Maker, and we do that which we were intended to do."

"I am glad that I let my thoughts wander during the song," said Helen. "I couldn't help but wonder just what my mission on Earth might be. I was trying desperately to think of something that I had been sent to Earth to do. It was during this time, that I received the answer. It came so quickly and unexpectedly that I was overwhelmed."

"I knew that you must have been wondering, when you told me that you had received your instructions," said Helen's mother. "It is a delightful experience."

They had been walking rather aimlessly down the street while they visited. Now they were within sight of their home, and Helen's mother said, "You have a little while remaining before you must return to Earth. Is there anything special you would like to do?"

"No," said Helen, "except to enjoy the beauty. There is a park ahead; shall we sit there and watch the people?"

"I think that would be better than going into the house on such a lovely Sunday as this," said her mother.

"All days are nice here," said Helen.

"Yes, but I think the coloring of the sky is especially pretty today; and there are so many people out for a stroll to watch," said her mother.

They had just seated themselves in the park, when Helen said, "Look who's coming!"

"Well of all things," said her father, "the whole family!"

"I guess they changed their minds and decided to see you off after all," said her mother.

"I dislike goodbyes," said Helen, "but I am glad to have a chance to see them again. I don't see the Grandparents though."

"Of all places to find you," said Uncle Henry, "sitting in

the park."

"Here are some roses I brought you," said Mary. "I have intended to bring them to you everyday, but didn't. At least you will have them for a little while before you return to Earth."

"Did you say roses: They look more like peonies to me, that is, in size. My but they are beautiful! Thank you, Mary," Helen said smelling the roses.

"We just had to come and see you again before you leave," said Aunt Linda sitting down beside Helen.

"Hello there, Uncle Frank!" said Helen. "Where are the grandparents?"

"They said to tell you that they were invited out for the afternoon and couldn't come, but they would be thinking of you," said Mary. "Sunday afternoons are usually a get together time here."

"Yep!" said Uncle Henry, "when we aren't visiting you folks on Earth on Sundays, when you are most apt to be home, we get together with our friends and families here."

"I'm glad you folks came anyway," said Helen. Are you going to Earth with me?"

"No, said Aunt Linda, "we will bid you goodbye here, and let your folks have these last few minutes alone with you."

"Got your suitcase all packed," asked Uncle Henry with a twinkle in his eye.

"Yes," said Helen, "the same one I had when I came."

"Well you don't want to forget anything," Uncle Henry said jokingly. "I guess all that I can take with me is what I have learned," said Helen laughing. I would like to take these flowers and this dress along though."

"Well now isn't that just like a woman? Thinks more about looking pretty, and making a grand entrance with a big bouquet of flowers, than she does about the knowledge she has gained," said Uncle Henry.

"But I have the knowledge anyway," said Helen, "so I might just as well wish for these things too."

"Well, Helen, I guess that Frank and I will bid you goodbye now. We have some people coming in for the afternoon and I'd hate to have them find us gone," said Aunt Linda as she kissed Helen goodbye.

"Goodbye Helen," said Uncle Frank. "Do I get a kiss too?"

"Why of course," said Helen.

"Think of us once in awhile," said Aunt Linda. "We'll miss you being here with us, but we'll keep an eye on you just the same."

As they left, Helen had her first pangs of saying goodbye. She was very quiet in the moment that followed their leaving. Soon this would all be a thing of the past. As long as she had to return to Earth and take up her life again, she was anxious to have her farewells over with.

"How much more time have I?" asked Helen uneasily.

"We haven't been summoned yet," said her father,, "but if you are getting uneasy, we can go anytime now and stand in readiness."

"No," said Helen, "I believe I will stay until we are summoned. It will be a long time before I come back again, and I will have lots of time to see the Earth. I want to have one more good look at all the beauty here, to take back in my mind's eye."

"It won't be any time at all," said Uncle Henry, until you are here again. Earth life is really very short; even though you spend a good many years there. In the long run, you spend a much longer time here. So go back without regret, and make the most of your life."

"Yes," said her father, "live a full and happy life and you'll not regret it. Remember Earth life is your preparing ground, which enables you to progress when you come over here. It is the cradle for your soul."

"Yes, but it is hard for a child to be returned to the cradle after it has once experienced being lifted from that cradle. That is very much the way I feel," said Helen. "But I suppose that once I am back there, I will settle down and be quite contented, just as a child who resigns to a nap in its cradle," Helen laughed.

"Here comes Trixie on the run," said Mary. He is coming at breakneck speed. I guess he wants to bid you goodbye too."

"A dog is a man's best friend," said Uncle Henry. "Well Trixie, you nearly missed the boat; but you made it and that is all that counts."

Trixie jumped up on Helen and in his excitement knocked the bouquet out of Helen's hand. Helen patted Trixie while Mary picked up the flowers for her.

"There," Helen said to Trixie, "See what you did. But seeing that you came to bid me goodbye, I'll forgive you," she said laughing and rumpling his fur."

"There is our beacon," said Helen's mother, "so we must be leaving now."

"I was looking for a thought projection," said Helen. "This sort of message is new to me."

"Some times a light such as this beckons us too," said her mother. "If we follow this beam, it will lead to the one who is calling us."

"It is rather like a rainbow," said Helen. It stops here in front of us, and as we look where it leads, it forms an arch like a pathway."

"That is what it is," said her father. "It serves as a pathway to the one who sent it."

"For the first time in my life I know what lies at the end of the rainbow," said Helen her eyes twinkling. "I have always wondered if there really was a pot of gold at the end of a rainbow. Now I know that Heaven is at one end, and Heaven on Earth at the other."

"Oh so now you admit that there is a Heaven on Earth," said Uncle Henry. "I thought a moment ago, the way you talked, that you looked upon Earth as ashes," he said teasingly.

"Well in a way it is," said Helen. "But remember Paul will be there to greet me and that will seem like Heaven. You know, after all, there is a bond between us, and I guess I will really be glad to talk to him again."

"Living true to form," said Uncle Henry. "Once a person decides to go home; he's like a horse headed for the barn. Just no stopping him."

"It's all in the mind," said Helen laughing. "As long as I knew I was to be here, I was happy and contented. Now I know I'm going back to be with Paul again, I find I'm getting quite excited about it."

"That's the right attitude to take!" said Uncle Henry giving her a great big hug. "Now don't forget to think of us once in awhile."

"You can be sure that I won't," said Helen. "Take good care of yourselves and Trixie."

"Here, let me put this flower in your hair," said Mary. "This one broke off when it fell. There, now you look elegant! Goodbye and good luck."

"Thank you," said Helen as she waved goodbye to them.

Chapter XV

Helen and her parents entered the hospital room where they found the doctor and Paul talking over Helen's condition.

The Doctors from Heaven were standing by the bed. "We waited to send for you until Paul and the Doctor arrived," one of them told Helen. "We want them both to be here when you rally from this coma."

"Is everything alright now?" Helen asked.

"Your body is in fine shape now," the Doctor said. "The blood clot has thoroughly dissolved. You can return any time now, and you will be perfectly well."

"I'm sure I don't know how to go about that," said Helen. "Just how will I get back?"

"When you are ready, you will return, just as you left it, without any special effort on your part," said the Doctor.

"Be sure you get in right side up," said her father laughing.

"My goodness!" said Helen, "Don't tell me I could make such a blunder as that. Wouldn't it be awful to be walking around on my head the rest of my Earth life," she laughed.

"There is no chance of that," said her mother. "You know the kind of remarks your father likes to make. And you should know better by this time, than to take him seriously."

"Will you be here awhile after I return to my body?" Helen asked as if that would be a comfort to her.

"Oh yes, we will remain for awhile," said her father. "We want to see just how you feel to be back again. And if there is to be a show, as you hinted, we wouldn't want to miss the fun.

"Well dear," said her mother, "Perhaps you had better get started before Paul and the Doctor decide to leave." "Yes," said the attending Doctor. "Any time now."

Helen looked at her parents for a full minute as though to have this picture to take with her. "Here mother take these flowers. I will keep the one in my hair, but I suppose it will be gone once I am back."

"Now," said her father, "Just relax and think that you are going to return to your body. That is all you need to do."

"Don't I have to hold my nose and make a dive as when plunging into the water?" asked Helen mischievously.

"No, nothing like that," laughed her mother. "Here give me a kiss."

Helen kissed her parents goodbye and hugged them tightly. I have really had a wonderful time," said Helen. "And I can never thank you enough for all you have shown me. Now I guess I had better go before my power light goes off," she laughed.

Before another word could be spoken, Helen had left their side. She had gone back to her physical body as quickly and easily as she had left it.

Helen's body moved a little on the bed in just a moment. The Doctor and Paul stepped to her side.

"By glory!" said the Doctor to Paul. "I believe Helen is rousing."

Helen wiggled as if to move away from something. "Goodbye folks" she mumbled. "I..made ..it. but..oh how heavy.. it seems. Like heavy and piled.. on me .. at the beach ... remember.. father.."

"She's coming to," said the Doctor. "Don't try to force her for awhile by talking to her. Just let her come out of it first."

"But she is talking so strangely," said Paul.

"That is only to be expected," said the Doctor. "She may be a bit confused for a few minutes, like coming out of ether; but don't let it upset you. She doesn't know what she is saying."

Helen stretched her neck and frowned. "Feels .. so..

hindersome.. and bulky," she said.

"Do you think something is hurting her?" asked Paul nervously.

"I don't know," said the Doctor, "we will ask her in a moment."

Now Helen smiled. "Tell.. your friends .. back there ..I made it .. before the ... light failed. "I'm getting.. used to.. my body.. again now.. It doesn't seem quite ... so heavy. I feel fine.. no hurt ... not tired."

The Doctor was taking Helen's pulse. "Her pulse seems fine,' he said. "A little time of quiet and she'll soon be alright I believe."

Helen opened her eyes now upon hearing these words. She was now conscious that she had been talking to her family out loud. She had been so concerned about being back in her body, that she had forgotten about the others in the room until now. She felt a little sheepish as she opened her eyes.

"Hello Paul!" she said. "Did you think I was never coming back?" she smiled at him.

"You are alright now," said Paul. "Just take it easy and don't try to talk. I'll sit here by you. You've been pretty sick, but you are alright now."

"Sick?" Helen said smiling dreamily. "No Paul, I haven't been sick, just my body."

Paul looked at the Doctor in alarm.

"Do you feel any pain in your head?" asked the Doctor. "Or any discomfort?"

"Nope," said Helen quite her old self now. "The blood clot has dissolved and I'm all fine."

The Doctor looked at Paul and then back at Helen. "What did you say?" he said, not able to believe his ears.

"I said the blood clot has dissolved and I can go home now," said Helen delighted with his amazement.

"This is the most remarkable thing I ever heard of," said the Doctor quite perplexed.

"Not remarkable," said Helen. "It's a miracle!"

"Helen, how did you know about this blood clot you have?" Paul asked anxiously.

"Blood clot I had!" corrected Helen. "It's all gone, just as I told you. Take an X-ray and see, if you don't believe it."

Helen pulled herself up to a sitting position and grinned impishly at them. "And don't tell me to lie down," she said. "This is not going to hurt me one bit, but get the stiffness out of my body. Why didn't you move me about more?"

"I'd rather you wouldn't move about so much yet," said the Doctor, until we see about that blood clot. You might cause yourself a relapse."

"No relapse," said Helen. "And no more pampering

myself from now on. All my old trouble has been cured too."

"Helen, this isn't like you," said Paul. You always do what the Doctor thinks best. Why, you act as though you know all about this sickness. Remember Dear, the Doctor knows the conditions that you have been under for the last few days, and therefore knows the dangers of your overdoing."

Helen smiled and patted his hand reassuringly. "Yes and so do I know what has been going on, and also, what isn't going on anymore, as you two suspect. I tell you the blood clot is gone or I wouldn't be talking to you like this and feeling so well.

"She has something there," said the Doctor. "It is true, that she wouldn't feel this well, if the pressure was still there. However, we will take a picture and make sure."

"Let's go do it right away," said Helen, "so I can go home tonight."

"You won't go home tonight anyway," said the Doctor. "But if the clot is gone, and you feel this way tomorrow, then you may go home."

"But tell me," said the Doctor, "How do you know so much about your condition?"

"You wouldn't believe me if I told you," Helen laughed. "But I will tell you nevertheless. I was conscious of everything that went on."

"Impossible!" said the Doctor.

"See, what did I tell you. I knew you wouldn't believe me," said Helen. "But it is true anyway."

"But you didn't respond to our talking to you," said Paul. "Could you hear, but couldn't answer?"

"I could hear and answer; but you couldn't hear me," said Helen. "I was out of my body and walking around this room. It was quite an experience."

"I should think it would be," laughed the Doctor. "You quiet down now or you will be experiencing it again. You certainly had queer dreams during your coma!"

"Dreams!" exclaimed Helen.

"Now don't excite yourself Helen," said Paul. "You can tell me all about it when you are real well again and home. I'll listen to you then, but now do be careful," he said pleadingly.

"I must get back to the office now," said the Doctor. By night when I see you again, you will be out of the fog."

"Or you will be more befogged," Helen called after him good naturedly.

Paul tried to keep Helen somewhat quiet, but she was all over the bed. He couldn't doubt that she was really feeling quite well as he watched her moving about, so happily.

It was mid-afternoon when Helen had X-ray pictures taken. Now she knew that she would soon be going home and take up her normal life again.

Helen saw that there was no use to try to make Paul and the Doctor believe her story so she decided to bide her time. Time would prove her story, but there was no use in causing them unnecessary anxiety now.

"Why are you feeling the side of your head, does it hurt?" Paul asked.

"I just remembered something," said Helen. "I had a flower in my hair when I came back, and I was wondering if it was still there. But it isn't. Too bad, it was such a beautiful flower."

Helen looked down at her gown. She had been so occupied with other things that she had forgotten about her lovely dress.

"Paul, would you believe me if I told you I had been to Heaven and seen my folks?"

"I don't know what to say," said Paul, "or to think. You have been saying such peculiar things that it almost leads me to believe that perhaps it wasn't just a dream."

"It wasn't any dream," said Helen. "I was just thinking about the dress I had on when I left there. I wish that you could have seen it. You would have liked it."

"I'm just glad to have you feeling well again," said Paul. "You look good to me just as you are."

"I was here several times with you Paul, but I guess I told you all about that. You still don't believe that such a thing is possible, do you?" Helen asked.

"I am beginning to think that anything is possible," said Paul lightly. "And I'll have to believe you if the X-rays bear you out."

The Doctor came in to see Helen around dinner time that evening, bringing the report of the X-ray findings.

"How has Helen been behaving this afternoon, Paul?" "I haven't been able to quiet her down much. She feels too good for her own good, I guess."

"Well no harm done, according to the X-ray report. I guess she knew what she was talking about. There isn't a trace of the clot left. Isn't that fine?" asked the Doctor relieved.

"Maybe you two will pay some attention to me from now on, and take my word," said Helen gaily. "Now will you let me go home tonight?"

"You might just as well," said Paul. "Or she will say I told you so, in the morning."

"Well it is entirely without precedent in my long practice, " but as I can offer no good sound reason for her remaining overnight under the circumstances, I believe I will give my consent and let her go home tonight," said the Doctor.

"And to repay you for being so generous," said Helen, "sometime I will tell you what actually happened during my coma. After you think that I have regained my normal state of mind," she laughed.

"So you are still suffering from delusions," said the Doctor. "In that case perhaps I had better keep you here after all."

"I have no delusions," said Helen. "But you and Paul seem to have your share of delusions about a great many things."

"Just like all crazy people!" said Paul winking at the Doctor. "Now she insists that she isn't crazy; but that we are."

"Well perhaps we should just pamper her and see if she gets over it," said the Doctor in mock seriousness.

"Supposing then that you begin by getting my clothes for me," said Helen, playing their little game.

"You won't need clothes," said the Doctor. "You don't think you are going to get up and walk out of here, do you?"

"Why not?" I feel fine," said Helen.

"You would find that regardless of your good feelings, that your legs would feel a bit wobbly," the Doctor told her. "No, you will use the wheel chair to get you to the car, and you can't talk me out of that."

"Well even at that, I can dress can't I?" Helen asked.

"Dress if you wish, but not walk," said the Doctor. Helen was dressed and ready in no time.

Paul had driven the car around to the Emergency entrance to make it easier to wheel Helen to the car from the elevator.

Now Paul and the Doctor placed her, in the wheel chair, and they were already to leave for home.

The Doctor gave Helen his final instructions regarding her conduct when she reached home. "And you better mind me," he said, or I'll never let you have your own way again. We don't want you to have another spell such as this, so take it easy, for awhile anyway."

I'll be a model patient," said Helen in an angelic tone.

The Doctor stopped by the doorway of another's patient room, and watched them go to the elevator. "It is a miracle," he said half under his breath.

Paul pushed the buzzer for the elevator and waited. Helen smiled up at him from her wheel chair.

The elevator stopped, and the doors opened. The attendant helped Paul with the wheel chair into the elevator.

"It will be wonderful to have you home again," Paul said as he turned the wheel chair around facing the door. "I was so afraid for awhile that you might die."

"Don't look so morbid when you speak of death," said Helen disapprovingly. "You speak of it as though it was the end of everything."

Paul looked at Helen bewildered. "Well how else is there to look at it?" he asked.

Helen smiled, and her eyes lit up with a merry twinkle. "Death," she said, "is the greatest adventure of life. it should be looked forward to with great anticipation, for it is an adventure into a world of reality, and more beauty than could be dreamed."

The elevator doors closed on Paul and Helen, taking her on her way back to complete her Earth life, well and happy in her new understanding and knowledge of Heaven and Earth.

The End

Moina's Heaven & Earth

Moina Morgan Vanderveer

Moina's Heaven & Earth

Moina Morgan Vanderveer